love, artifacts, and you

SARAH READY

ALSO BY SARAH READY

Stand Alone Romances:

The Fall in Love Checklist

Hero Ever After

Josh and Gemma Make a Baby

Soul Mates in Romeo Romance Series:

Chasing Romeo

Love Not at First Sight

Romance by the Book

Love, Artifacts, and You

Find these books and more by Sarah Ready at:

www.sarahready.com/romance-books

Sign up to receive bonus content, exclusive epilogues and more at:
www.sarahready.com/newsletter

artifacts, and ever-present danger. Soon, they're confronted with a choice, what is the greater treasure – true love or revenge?

W.W. CROWN BOOKS
An imprint of Swift & Lewis Publishing LLC
www.wwcrown.com

Library of Congress Control Number: 2021919069
ISBN: 978-1-954007-23-9 (eBook)
ISBN: 978-1-954007-24-6 (pbk)
ISBN: 978-1-954007-25-3 (large print)
ISBN: 978-1-954007-26-0 (hbk)

love, artifacts, and you

1

———

ANDREW

I LIFT THE *HEART OF THE EMPRESS* FROM ITS WATERY TOMB AND lock my eyes, not on the gemstone, but on Emma. Her eyes reflect the glow of the lanterns, and the sparkle of the world's largest pigeon blood ruby.

"We found it," she whispers. Her awe-filled voice echoes around the rocky limestone walls of the cenote.

We found it.

She reaches toward me, her fingers hang in the air, five feet away at the edge of the murky pool. She's in dirt-caked cargo pants, a long-sleeved shirt and boots, and she's covered in cobwebs and cave muck. I feel a smile curve on my lips. And it's because I know she's reaching for me, not for the two-hundred-karat ruby I'm holding above the water.

The *look* on her face. It makes me hungry, makes me think of kissing her, of laying under the stars in the humid, sap-scented heat and kissing her lips.

We did it.

My Uncle Rigo lets out a ragged yell of astonishment. "You did it, boy. You did it! Your mother, she's watching over you. She sent you this luck. You've the golden touch, boy. The golden touch!" He whips around to Edward Castleton, Emma's father. "What did I tell you? My nephew is a bloodhound. You owe us more than the porter's fee, Castleton. Much more."

"Let me see it," says Castleton in a hard, whip-like voice. The hair on the back of my neck stands on end and I itch to look behind me.

Emma breaks my gaze and looks toward Castleton. "Dad?"

"Give it to me, boy," he snaps.

I carefully step over the bottom of the pool and wade toward the water's edge. The closer I get to shore, the heavier the ruby feels in my hand. Castleton watches the gem with flinty, steel-hard eyes.

My uncle claps his hands and chuckles to himself.

I glance down at the *Heart of the Empress*. She looks just like the drawings in Cortez's journals. A ten-inch heart made of solid gold, covered in emeralds, sapphires, diamonds, hundreds of gemstones, and at the center a two-hundred-karat blood red ruby.

Men would kill for this. My skin goes cold but I brush the thought aside.

Not these men.

I've been with Castleton for thirteen years, since I was four years old. My guardian, Uncle Rigo, is his porter. We haul his luggage, set up camp, cook his meals, take care of his travel arrangements, ease the way with locals, and sometimes, like on this trip, help with the hunt.

For the past three months we've been sleeping at the edge of this cenote, a twisting underground cavern that opens like a gaping mouth into the thick rainforest. We're in conquistador territory of centuries past—a two-day hike to the nearest village.

Every day we followed the maze of the watery labyrinth described in Cortez's journal. Left, right, right, left at the cross, right at the spider rock, left. Then, dive into the pool at the heart of the cavern, murky as an uncut gem.

The floor of the pool, fifteen feet down, was jagged like the shards of a broken glass strewn over a muddy floor. For days, I dove to the bottom. I'd pull in a breath and kick my way down into the murky green water lit only by my dim waterproof headlamp. I dredged the bottom and searched the shallow cracks, until finally, I found her. The *Heart*.

I step onto the solid gray limestone floor of the cave. The cold water sluices from my clothing and makes a puddle at my feet. I shake the water off my face and out of my eyes. Castleton and my uncle crowd me at the edge of the pool. Emma stands on her tiptoes behind them. She's always complaining that five-foot-two is an unfair height. She hops up and down, but I bet she still can't see. I'll hear about it later. The thought makes me smile and takes away the last vestiges of foreboding.

"Let's see it," Castleton says. He holds out his hands. They're perfectly smooth, bone white, with round, clean nails.

My hands, wrapped around the *Heart*, are tanned and chapped, with broken nails that seem permanently encrusted with dirt. No matter how often I clean them, the next day, I work and they're dirty again.

I set the heavy artifact in his clean hands.

He lets out a long sigh, like the sigh you give after watching the last orange of the sunset slip under the sea.

"The *Heart of the Empress*." His voice reverberates in the cave.

He holds up the stone to the lantern's light, and even coated in centuries of grime, the blood ruby still glows, just as it must have in Queen Isabella's court.

My uncle chuckles the hearty, happy laugh he reserves for lost artifact finds. "My nephew! Your son recovered the Empress's Heart, what do you think of that, Celia?" he asks. "I may only be a porter, but someday, someday soon, your son will be someone. Someone!" He's talking to my mom, his only sister, dead for thirteen years now. He does it when he's overwhelmed with emotion or head-cracking drunk. Right now, he's overwhelmed.

I look over Rigo's shoulder at Emma and wink.

She pushes her long thick bangs out her eyes and shares a smile of happiness and laughter.

We did it.

My uncle is still talking, "He's an artifact bloodhound, he is. We're talking partnership. Fifty-fifty split."

Castleton says something in response.

I don't listen. I don't care about the find. That's for Castleton and my uncle. Let them worry about money and fees and partnerships. None of that matters to me.

What do I want?

Emma.

Emma and me together. Kissing under the stars.

Tonight, Emma mouths at me.

I give a subtle nod of my head.

Tonight.

I sneak through the inky tropical darkness. The insects and the night creatures howl and whine, covering up any noise I could make. It's nearing midnight. Castleton and my uncle stayed up late, drinking and toasting each other around the flickering fire. They passed the *Heart of the Empress* back and forth with the liquor bottle.

I cleaned up, made dinner and started to pack up camp. We'll be leaving tomorrow, or the next day at the latest. We'll head to the city, where Castleton will get the ruby to the proper channels. Then we'll head to the airport, and to the location of our next hunt.

Except for Emma, she'll fly back to New Hampshire for her final year of private school. Tonight might be our last night together for another ten months. I rub at my chest, I've always hated it when she leaves for school.

For the last eight years, Emma's spent summers with her dad at base camp. Which meant she spent them with me. Summers are my favorite time of year, no matter where I am in the world. Because summer means Emma.

I press my fingers to the flap of her tent and listen. There's no noise from inside. There's only the loud night whir of the forest. Maybe she's already asleep? Then, her hand reaches out of the tent and grabs my calf. She yanks me down and I roll through the low entrance. My breath rushes out in a sharp oomph.

Laying on the nylon covered ground, I stare up at the peak of Emma's tent. The full moon shines through the blue fabric and gives the tent a soft luminescent glow. Emma scrambles on all fours toward me and her face appears over mine. I have enough light to make out the freckles sprinkled over her nose and cheeks, even the one just above her lip that makes me want to kiss her every time I see it. When I first saw her, I was ten, and I thought those freckles meant she'd be trouble. I was right.

"Took you long enough," she whispers. Then her mouth spreads into a wide grin.

I take a deep breath and pull in the smell of castor soap, bug spray, and loamy forest.

"They stayed up late celebrating," I say.

Castleton and my uncle don't know that Emma and I meet at night. When we were younger we had the run of the camp. As long as my chores were done we could play or swim or dig or run free. But the year Emma turned fourteen, Castleton turned a disapproving eye on our friendship. And Uncle Rigo gave me *the talk*. Emma was not for me.

The disapproving stares from Castleton and my uncle's talk kept us apart when they were around. But, every other minute of the day we stuck together.

"They were discussing partnership," I say. I sit up and lean against Emma's raised cot. She settles in next to me.

"Good. They should. You've been instrumental in every find since the *USS Seafarer* and that was three years ago," she says. "If I had my way, you'd have been partner years ago."

I shrug and she shoves at my shoulder.

"Don't shrug at me. You have so much potential. You could be the greatest archeologist in the world. You have so much knowledge and more experience than most tenured professors. I don't understand why you don't want more."

She pauses, then climbs up onto her cot. I follow her and spread out next to her. It feels sinful to lay in a bed with her. My hand aches to reach out and touch her.

"What would I do with more?" I ask. "More makes people miserable. I see it all the time, in every country I've visited. The more people have, the more miserable they are. Once you get more—more prestige, more money, you spend the rest of your life chasing even more of it and being terrified you'll lose all of it. No thank you."

Emma lets out a short huff. She rolls on her side and looks at me. Her eyes are wide, deep pools in the moonlight. "So what do you want? What would make you happy?" she asks.

I stare at the freckle above her lip and ache for it.

Emma licks her lower lip and I hold back a groan. Her eyes go dark.

"Do you remember when we first met?" she asks. She reaches out and brushes her fingers across my jaw. My heart beats wildly in response.

"You said I was a barbarian," I say with a smile.

"A Visigoth," she says.

"That's right. I remember." A Visigoth, to nine-year-old Emma, was a horrible insult, since the Visigoths sacked Rome and destroyed all its treasures. The Visigoths left the jewel of the Roman empire a smoking ruin, a shell of its former self.

She nods. "But then my dad told me if I didn't like you he'd fire your uncle and send you away. He told me if you ever displeased me, he'd send you both back to the third-world slum he found you in—back to picking pockets and sniffing glue fumes off your hands."

"Really pleasant," I say.

I'd heard the story from her before. The years before my uncle took me in are a hazy blur. I remember my mom begging on a street corner, and hunger so intense it became a consuming monster. I remember stealing tourists' wallets for a man who in return gave me a coin and a splatter of glue on my hands. I'd inhale the fumes to numb the hunger. Then one morning my mom was gone. Someone sent word to my uncle. At age four, I became his ward. No one could find my father, an American I'd never met.

Then Dr. Castleton found us. He realized I spoke six languages fluently, a survival mechanism learned from conning tourists. He learned that my uncle had a broad back and the ability to navigate any circumstance, and he decided to bring us along on his hunts.

Emma raises her eyebrows. "My dad's protective."

"Yes," I agree.

She frowns and touches her fingertips to my jaw, featherlight. My heart speeds up.

"I decided that day that I'd do everything in my power to like you." Her lips twitch, then curve into a smile. "There'd be nothing to stop me from becoming your best friend, so my dad would never send you away."

"I made it hard," I say.

"You were terrible."

"I thought you were a snotty princess."

"I am," she says. She lets out a happy laugh.

I lean forward and brush my lips over hers. Her laugh cuts off with a gasp. Then her fingers slide up my jaw, to my cheek, through my hair. I taste her, wood-smoke and mint, fresh water and jungle. She's the one thing, the only thing on earth that I've ever wanted *more* of. Emma is my *more*.

She pulls her mouth away. I reach for her and she pushes me away.

"You didn't answer my question."

My brain is fuzzy, I can't remember her question.

"What will make you happy?" she asks.

I look at her, bathed in filtered moonlight, laying on her cot, in the cocoon of her small tent, and my chest is so full.

"You," I say in a low voice.

She takes in a sharp breath. "I've decided. I'm not going to Oxford."

I stare at her in shock. She looks back resolutely.

"What? No. That's your dream. You'll go to Oxford, get your PhD, run Castleton once your dad retires, sit on the boards of a thousand museums around the world..." The last is a joke, but not by much.

"It's not my dream if I can't do it with you," she says. "None of it matters if you're not there too."

I'm not going to Oxford. We both know it. No university in

the world would accept me. A boy, born in an alley, pulled off the streets, who's never gone to school, who could barely sit still long enough to learn to read and write. My mother never learned to read, my uncle only knows how to sign his name. No, university isn't for me.

"I'll be here." I gesture around the tent, meaning that I'll be with her father on the hunt. "I'll wait for you."

She shakes her head. "After I graduate high school, I'll start at Oxford. There'll be no time to come back. My dad is already talking about it. Summer classes, internships, tours, straight through until I get my PhD. He won't let me back on the hunt. I won't see you. Not for six years, eight years, maybe more. I can't do it. I won't."

There seems to be less air in the tent when I think of the years she won't be here. But still.

"You're seventeen," I say, "Don't throw your future away."

When my uncle gave me the talk, he told me that Emma wasn't for me. That she belonged to a boy in America. A boy that went to a school like hers, that had a family pedigree like hers, that had old money and culture like her. A boy that matched her and raised her up. Not one that brought her down.

I didn't understand him until now.

If Emma gives up Oxford, or going to university to stay with me, she'll be stuck. Just like the ruby was stuck at the bottom of the pool, no one will be able to see Emma shine, or see her brilliance. I'd bury her light.

"You're seventeen too," she says, and she pushes at my shoulder. I let out a grunt. "Don't tell me you don't know what you want."

I can't, she knows I can't.

I've always wanted her.

"We both know you have better things waiting for you," I say.

She nods. "I have things waiting. A big old creaky estate built back in 1792. A fancy degree from one of the best schools in the world. Charity galas, museum exhibit openings."

I picture her in a ballgown under the golden chandeliers of a museum exhibit hall. The dress is tight over her chest and frothy like sea foam around her hips. It's like the formal dress in the photo she showed me from her debutante ball. She glows amidst the gold-streaked marble columns in my mind.

"I have lots of things waiting," she says. "But I'd rather be with you in a tent, dirty and exhausted after a day of digging than anywhere else in the world."

I close my eyes and picture what that would look like.

"Your dad would disown you," I say.

"Probably. I bet he wants me to marry Justin Van Cleeve."

My eyes open and I stare at the ceiling, trying to remember what the Van Cleeve kid looked like. He was her escort to the debutante ball. Blond wavy hair, a dimple in his chin, tall, moneyed, wore the formal suit like he'd been in one plenty of times before. A twinge of irritation flashes through me.

I'm the antithesis of Van Cleeve. I have thick black hair, brown eyes so dark they look black, sun dark skin, and jeans and long t-shirts washed so many times I can't remember their original color.

"So after your dad disowns you, then what?" I ask.

She grins at me. "We live out of our tent."

"How will we get food, money?"

"We could live near a tourist archeological site. Maybe somewhere near here. You'd be a translator, I'd be a guide. At dusk, you'd go out and catch fish. I'd find fruit, fresh mango. We'd cook our food over the fire. Then we'd sit under the stars. You'd be tired, so I'd rub your back. I'd be sleepy, so you'd hold me close. Then we'd go in our tent and lay down on our cot."

"We'd be married?" I ask.

"Mhmm," she says.

"We'd be poor," I say.

"Rich in love."

My breath catches. She's never said she loves me. I've never told her.

I inch my hand over the cot and find her fingers. I take her hand in mine and gently squeeze.

The thought is as appealing as the siren songs of ancient Greece. I want what she's describing so badly.

"Someday, we'll start our own business, Santiago and Castleton. You heard your uncle, you're a bloodhound. I'll find the dig sites, you'll find the artifacts. We'll be unstoppable."

I hear a twig snap outside the tent. Both of us tense and go quiet. We've always been careful to never be caught. We stay still and silent for a minute, two, finally I relax.

"It was nothing," I say.

She nods, then she leans closer. "I was thinking…"

"What?"

"Have you ever wondered…"

"What?" My heart thuds at the low tone of her voice.

She takes a deep breath. "Have you ever wondered…what it would be like to make love?"

I go hard in half a second and grow dizzy as the blood rushes from my head.

Holy ever loving…

I'd trade a thousand rubies to hear her say that again.

"Emma…"

She wrinkles her nose. "Oh. You haven't."

"Emma—"

She shifts and moves to get up from the bed.

"Sorry," she says. "I just thought…we were talking about—"

I grab her arm and pull her down. She lands on top of me and the cot shudders under us. She wiggles against me and I know the moment she feels how hard I am because she goes completely still. Her eyes go wide and she pulls in a sharp breath.

"Oh," she whispers.

I feel like I'm on fire. The only thing I can concentrate on is where her warm body presses into mine. She relaxes further into me and slowly, slowly, I wrap my arms around her back and imprison her against me.

She stretches out over me and drags herself along my length. I groan at the flash of agony. Then I draw in a breath and thrust up toward her. She sends her hands to my shoulders and presses her lips to my jaw.

My word.

"I'll come back," she says. She rocks against me. "After I graduate. I won't go to university. I'll come back to be with you."

"I'll wait for you," I promise. "I want you to go to university. I want you to meet your potential. I'll wait." Forever, I'd wait forever.

I can barely think. I want more than anything to make love to her, to strip her naked and make love under the stars.

Another twig snaps. Then another.

The fog clears from my mind and the hair on the back of my neck stands on end for the second time in twenty-four hours. The forest has gone completely quiet.

I stiffen and push up onto my forearms.

The forest only goes quiet when there's a predator nearby.

"What is—"

"Shhh." I press my hand to her lips.

I roll off Emma and silently come to my feet. I have to crouch in her tent. I step carefully toward the entrance. When I'm there I pause and gesture at Emma to stay back.

I have a machete in my tent. Castleton has a gun for protection against wild animals. Something is here. I can feel it in the way the silent jungle holds its breath, like a jaguar right before it jumps.

Emma materializes next to me. "What is it?" she whispers.

I shake my head.

"Stay he—"

The sharp crack of a gunshot thunders through the silence.

Emma screams.

I grab her, clamp my hand over her mouth.

A man yells. Another gunshot. I hear my uncle scream. It's hoarse and full of pain. A thick fiery fear burns through me.

Someone's here. They're here for the ruby, or for us, or...I don't know. But they're here to hurt us.

I take Emma's hand and drag her through the camp. We run low, close to the ground, sprint toward the thick trees and vines. At the trees, I push Emma in, usher her toward the low, fat-leafed bushes.

"Hide. Get in," I say.

Another gunshot cracks in the night. My uncle screams again. There's shouting, the sound of fists hitting flesh and garbled words.

"Run, get out, run!" That's Castleton. He's screaming, and then, he's cut off.

Emma gasps. The whites of her eyes glow with fear in the moonlight.

"Get in, get in." I push her under the thick bushes. No one will see us under them.

Castleton shouts out again, a garbled, pained noise.

"Andrew!" she cries.

There's the beating of feet on the ground. The shouts of at least a dozen men. One sends out a call. A flashlight spears the darkness behind me. I've been seen. I have a split second to make a decision.

I hold Emma's eyes. Maybe for the last time. But if I can run back, draw them away from her, then…it's worth it.

There's a flash of some emotion I can't name in her eyes.

"No!" she cries.

"Yes," I say.

I yank the bushes down and sprint through the undergrowth back to camp. The men at the tree line chase after me. There's at least eight on my tail. I jump over the hot coals of the fire. The heat singes my pants. My tent is less than ten feet away, the machete just inside the entrance. I can grab it and lead the men deeper into the forest, farther from Emma.

I see my uncle, bathed in darkness, prone on the ground. Two men stand over him.

I hear another guttural yell from across camp. Castleton?

I dive to the entrance of my tent. I shove the flaps aside, grasp the handle of the machete and swing around.

I see too many things at once.

The man over my uncle cocks his gun and aims at my uncle's still body.

Castleton is shoved toward the light of the fire.

The group of men surrounds me in a tight semi-circle.

I see everything as if it's a still life, or a memory, and I'm no longer living this life. I see it as if I'm standing outside of myself. A numbing chill sweeps over me and pulls me back into myself.

I raise the machete in front of me, like a prayer. As if a single blade used to chop through jungle growth can save us all.

Please.

I count thirteen men.

What have they done to my uncle, to Emma's father? What will they do to us?

The man above my uncle pulls the trigger. My uncle jerks but doesn't make a sound.

They won't let us live.

I shout and run at the man in front of me. I swing the blade, readying for it to cut into flesh.

A shot sounds.

Before the noise stops, a burning agony rips through me. I fall forward, crash to the ground. The machete buries itself in my thigh.

They shot me. They...

A scream rips through the night.

Emma.

My Emma.

Blackness roars over me in consuming, searing pain.

⁓

Six Months Later

I tear through the jungle, ripping vines and thorns away with bleeding hands. I can hear them behind me. The men—I call them the wardens—chase me down. Each labored breath is a jagged knife in my lungs. I've lost at least thirty pounds in the last months. I've no muscle or flesh left to power me. I'm running on will alone.

My uncle is dead. They killed him yesterday when he was too feverish and weak to enter the mines. For weeks I'd been dragging him in the mine behind me, giving him half of my finds so he'd live long enough for us to escape—I'd stopped waiting for help to come months ago.

In the mines we're chained together, six in a group, the metal lengths bind us as we crawl deep into the stagnant hell where we search for stones. If you don't bring out quota, you're beaten. If you can't walk to go in, you die.

Every day that Uncle Rigo didn't find anything, I'd give him enough stones to keep him safe. He never healed properly from the gunshot wounds. Six months ago, I was young and still healthy, I was well within a week. "Your mother, she's watching over you," he'd say. "She's your angel. That Emma too, she's well, you'll see. Your mother will keep you safe."

I didn't remind him that my mother didn't keep me safe on the streets when she was alive. What could she do when she was dead?

I hold onto the prayer that Emma is alive. That she escaped. That she's safe and not in another hell, like this one. After they took me and my uncle, they drove us south for days, bound and blindfolded in the back of an SUV, until we reached the mines. Hell.

I crash through a thicket full of stinging vines and thorn-covered trees. I stumble and catch myself on a tree trunk. An inch-long spike pierces my palm. I let the pain clear my head. A shot of adrenaline pumps through me.

They're only fifty yards behind me. Gaining.

I veer to the right. I can see light. The sky. I haven't seen the clear blue of the sky in so many months. I go in the mine before sunrise and come out after dark. The blinding blue spurs me on. I'll reach it. I'll find help. Emma.

I race into the clearing. The sunlight blinds me. I blink at my surroundings as my heart thunders in my chest.

Run, it says, run. Get away.

There's a dirt track ahead, a mud-slicked SUV pulls in front of me.

I shout out.

The SUV stops. Blocking the road past.

The door opens. Crudell steps out. A vicious smile spreads across his face.

"Well. Well, well, well," he says.

Red covers my vision, blinding out the blue sky, the sun, my freedom.

Crudell is the cruelest, most sadistic man I've ever known. And yesterday he killed my uncle. I let out the noise of a wild animal. I rush him.

He raises his arm and hits me across the head with his club.

ONE YEAR LATER

CRUDELL'S FIST SMASHES INTO MY NOSE. I FEEL THE BONE BREAK. My eyes sting and white spots flash in my vision. Blood rushes out of my nose and it starts to swell. I pull in air through my mouth and taste the coppery blood dripping from my nostrils.

"How many now?" asks Crudell.

I squat against the wall of his office, a shabby wooden structure with two small windows and a coveted portable air conditioner. There's a corkboard on the wall with a yellowed map of the mine thumbtacked in place. Crudell catches me looking at it and hits me again.

I shake away the dizziness.

I lean against the wood. My wrists are cuffed together and looped into a large metal screw in the wall.

"How many?" he asks.

"Six," says the man I call Bigfoot. Mainly because I've never heard his name and he always kicks the people who don't move fast enough.

Six refers to the number of times I've tried, and failed, to escape.

"I should kill you," says Crudell.

I watch the expression on his face. He wants to, but for some reason he won't.

Blood runs backward from my nose down my throat. I spit onto the termite-gnawed gray wood floor.

"You're right," says Crudell. "I can't. I'm paid one hundred thousand dollars to keep you alive."

My head snaps up. I look at him. What's he saying?

He studies the swelling of my face. Then, "That's right. Every year you live, here, with me, I get a hundred thousand more." He smiles his snakelike smile.

One hundred thousand? For me? To keep me in this hell?

"Ah, I have your attention," he says, pleased with himself. "Ask me," he says. He leans back against his desk, a metal monstrosity rust-stained from years of sitting in jungle humidity.

I don't ask him. I made it a rule on the day I met him to never engage in conversation. He holds out his long-fingered hands. "Yes, exactly, you want to know who pays me to keep you."

I turn my attention away from him to the map on the wall. Maybe there's another way out I haven't found.

"Emma Castleton," he says.

I don't register the name at first, it sounds so different coming from him. But slowly it sinks in. Against my will, I turn back to him.

My eyes sting and my vision blurs.

"What did you do to her?" I snarl, breaking my own long-held rule. "Where is she? If you've hurt her I'll kill you. I'll—"

Crudell laughs as if this is the funniest thing he's ever heard, and then Bigfoot joins him.

Crudell dabs at his face with a red bandana then shoves it

back into the pocket of his shirt. The smile fades from his face, like it was never there. He walks around his desk, opens a drawer, pulls out a manila folder and drops it onto the desk's cluttered surface.

"I wondered," he says, "how, even though you can barely stand upright..."—he looks over my bony and starved frame—"how you keep escaping. Then I realized..." He snaps his fingers and holds up a piece of paper. "You still have hope. Hope is power. Maybe you thought the girl was your friend?"

I grit my teeth together.

"Or you thought you loved her?" He watches me carefully, then his eyes glint and he lets out a low laugh. "Oh, that's delicious. You did."

He walks in front of me and holds the paper up a foot from my face.

I won't look. I won't.

But I do.

It's the copy of a deposited check. One hundred thousand dollars, signed in elegant, flowing cursive, *Emma Marie Castleton*.

My stomach twists, refuses to accept it.

I lunge at Crudell. The handcuffs, looped into the screw on the wall, jerk me back.

I'll escape. What has he done to her? I'll get out and I'll kill him.

Two Years Later

Eighteen attempts.
All failed.

I lay on the termite-gnawed floor of Crudell's office.

The rough wood scratches my face. Sweat trickles down my forehead and mixes with the blood from my broken lip. I close my eyes and savor the coolness of the floor against my skin. I heave in another breath. Outside, the night is pitch black but the darkness does nothing to remove the oppressive heat.

Crudell squats down next to me.

"Another check from Miss Castleton," he says. I hear the paper crinkle as he waves it in front of me. "Look at it," he demands.

I open my eyes. See the date. Two years, it's been two years. I see her signature.

"What have you done to her?" I ask. They're the first words I've spoken to him in a year.

I dream of her. Picture her taken, blackmailed, scared.

Crudell's eyes flash. Surprise. He's surprised.

"Ah," he says. "I didn't realize."

He walks over to his desk. I take the time to close my eyes and dream of water. Cold water. Being clean. Sunlight. A table full of food, crispy bacon, crusty bread, a cold, juicy slice of watermelon. Chocolate ice cream with chocolate chips sprinkled on top.

An image of Emma, the freckles sprinkled over her cheeks and nose, flashes in my mind. She smiles at me and I dream of kissing the freckle over her mouth.

"Here. This should clear matters up for you," says Crudell.

I open my eyes, come back to the present of aching bones, gnawing hunger and eternal thirst. It takes me a moment to understand what Crudell is showing me.

It's a magazine. There's a glossy photo as part of an article.

I blink, make my eyes focus on the image. It's a woman holding the...the *Heart of the Empress*. The woman smiles at someone off camera. Not me, she's not smiling at me.

My chest constricts and I feel as if I'm back in the depths of the mine. In the dark. There's a howling in my ears.

The caption reads, Miss Emma Castleton donates forty-million-dollar artifact to the Metropolitan Museum, receives accolades.

The howling in my ears becomes a whine, a whimper, then builds again.

"Take me back," I growl.

"What's that?" asks Crudell.

The picture goes blurry. Who's she smiling at?

She's not scared. She's not hurt. She's glowing. Happy. More beautiful than before.

The howling drowns out everything else.

I hit my fists against the wood floor.

Slam. Slam. Slam.

"Take me back to the mine. Take me back."

I need the darkness.

THREE YEARS LATER

NO ESCAPE ATTEMPTS IN THE LAST YEAR.

Crudell has another check for one hundred thousand dollars.

He brings me to his office.

Shows me articles and photographs.

Emma at a gala dancing with Justin Van Cleeve.

Emma at a museum opening with her father. Yes, he's alive.

Emma. Justin. More Emma. Her father. Emma.

Hope turns to hate.

~

22

THE MINE PRESSES DOWN ON ME. THE FIVE PEOPLE CHAINED behind me claw at the walls. Tonight. I'm going to escape tonight. Five years. I've been in this hell for five years.

Crudell is dead. Dengue took him last week.

I'll miss his little photo parades of Emma.

I grin into the darkness. I know I look terrifying when I smile. Mostly because when I bare my teeth the others always scramble away from me or hastily perform the sign of the cross.

This mine has stripped the humanity from me.

No. She did.

Because she and her father wanted the *Heart*.

They wanted *more*.

I let out a low, scratchy laugh. The people behind me pause, wait to see if I've lost my mind. When I don't do anything else they start digging again.

I want more now too.

Tonight, I'll escape this hell and when I do I'll destroy her. I'll make her pay for every second of suffering, every ounce of pain. I'll destroy her life and everything she loves. I swear on my mother, on my uncle, on God.

I'll destroy Emma Castleton.

I'll ruin her.

I'll make her wish she'd never, ever laid eyes on me.

I'll make her pay.

I'll be the Visigoth to her Rome. I'll leave her a smoldering, smoking ruin. A heart of ashes. She named me right all those years ago. I'll be her destruction.

2

———

I drop my beat-up canvas duffel bag on the knotty pine floor of the old 1930s three-season cabin and look around at my new home. Three-season means that this old place is going to be uninhabitable come winter. But that's alright, beggars can't be choosers, and I've dropped below beggar status. The duffel bag contains all my worldly possessions, a few pairs of jeans, shirts, a pair of boots, my excavation tools, notebooks, and a few pencils filched from the golf pro counter at Justin's country club.

"What do you think?" Justin asks. He walks through the low pine-framed door. The wood has taken on an orange hue with age. He has two brown paper grocery bags in his arms. The bags are full of enough beans, rice, peanut butter and powdered milk to last me at least two weeks. He insisted on buying groceries and some cleaning supplies at the quaint grocery store in town.

"I love it," I say. And I mean it.

It has a roof and a door and a bed. That means I love it.

"I didn't realize it was quite so worn-down when I offered for you to stay here," Justin says. As of two days ago, I'm homeless, and Justin came to my rescue. He sets the groceries on the low varnished wooden counter. A layer of dust floats up into the air and then slowly settles back down.

The kitchen, like the rest of the one-room cabin, hasn't been updated since it was built in 1939. The cabin is on a small plot of land at the edge of Romeo, New York's state forest. The walls are made of wide pine logs. The front door leads right into the kitchen. There are three kitchen cabinets painted faded yellow and trimmed in blue, and the floors are red and white checkered linoleum tiles, some are cracked and peeling at the corners, but it's mostly intact. A tall blue pie cupboard stands against the wall next to a white ceramic sink. On the counter is a gas camp stove. There's no refrigerator, just an old ice-chest. But there is a black cat clock hanging on the wall. The type that swings its tail to count the seconds.

I wander to the living room. The carpet is matted dark brown and when I step on it the smell of must and engine grease fills the air. There's a brown fabric recliner, probably from the 1980s, in the center of the room. A cane with a brass eagle on top leans against its armrest. A TV dinner tray holds a TV guide from 1997 and a remote for the old tube TV across the room. There are a few cobweb-covered wooden shelves on the walls filled with dozens of decorative plates and ceramic-handled spoons that name tourist destinations—Las Vegas, The Grand Canyon, Everglades National Park.

The only other item in the room is a stained twin mattress on the floor with a gray blanket wadded at its base. The mattress is in the back corner under a small window. I walk to it and look out at the yard. There's a small meadow full of tall silver grass that within five yards meets the edge of the forest. But in the grass there's an overgrown cement block-lined firepit, a long-handled water pump, and, yes, a wooden outhouse.

"I was wondering where the bathroom was," I say. I smile and turn to Justin. He walked up behind me a few seconds ago.

For some reason, I like this cabin. It makes me feel a spark of something I can't name. The little town, Romeo, did too. I liked it.

He shakes his head. "No. No. That's it. You came. You saw. Now you can come back to the city and stay with me." He puts his hands over my arms and squeezes. "You're not staying here. When I learned my uncle left me his hunting cabin I didn't realize it was a heap of rot that should be demolished. I never should've offered for you to stay here. Stupid, idiotic idea."

"It's not that bad," I say.

He squeezes my arms and his lips lift in a sardonic smile. "Em, there are saplings growing from the roof, there's a family of mice living in the ice-chest, there's no bathroom—"

I jerk my head toward the outhouse.

"No indoor bathroom. And that mattress is something out of a horror movie." He lets go of my arms and takes my hand. He rubs my left ring finger and I swallow a lump.

"I'll be fine," I say in a chipper voice. "Remember, I spent my childhood living out of a tent. I've slept in much worse."

"Em," he says. There's a sad, resigned note in his voice.

I take my eyes away from the window and look up at Justin. Really look at him.

His face is as familiar to me as my own. Clear, forthright, blue-gray eyes, neatly trimmed wavy blond hair, a straight nose and chiseled jaw that represent generations of breeding wealth with good looks. Lips that turn up at the corners. Justin is always on the verge of a smile. He was born into wealth and privilege, just like me. Our mothers were best friends, they spent their summers together on Martha's Vineyard. He could've turned out rotten and entitled, but he didn't. He's honest and generous. And for the last nine years, he's been my closest friend.

"I can't," I say.

He searches my eyes and then drops my hand. He runs his fingers through his hair. It ruffles then falls flat again. He's in a navy pinstripe suit. He left his law office early to drive me here and didn't take the time to change. He's partner in his family's firm, the legal giant of New York City.

"Please come back with me," he says. "This was a mistake."

I start to shake my head no but he continues. "I'll have a guestroom made up, you can have the whole second floor to yourself." Justin lives in a four-story townhouse near the American Museum of Natural History. He got it for a steal— eight million dollars. I always suspected he bought it because he knew I haunted the halls of the museum almost daily. We've had a ritual for nearly five years that I stop by and stay for dinner anytime I'm at the museum.

"I won't ask you to marry me again," he says in a quiet voice.

I look down at the brown carpet. Last week Justin asked me to marry him.

"You asked for time to think, and I'll give you as long as you need."

"I know," I say. "It's not that."

Justin lets out a ragged sigh. "It'll blow over," he says. "It'll be forgotten by Christmas."

He may believe it. In fact, I can see in his eyes that he does, but he hasn't seen what I have. It won't blow over. The name Castleton is now synonymous with cheating, lying, morally and financially bankrupt scum.

I've always been honest with Justin. At least, I have since the night of the charity gala nine years ago, when he found me sobbing in a side room, right before I was to present the *Heart of the Empress*. He patted my back, listened to my half-sobbed, mostly indecipherable story about a boy I loved who was now dead, nearly a year gone and dead, and he told me that he'd stay with me. He said he wasn't adventurous, or interesting, and that he'd never run into a jungle, so I could count on him to be boring and around whenever I felt like crying. That he'd be fine if I just wanted to sit next to him and scowl.

He was calm, and forthright, and didn't expect anything of me at all.

My father expected me to forget Andrew, Rigo, the jungle. He wanted me to learn the ropes of running the family business. He immersed me in everything I'd ever need to know to be as successful as him. It was like he was possessed.

I barely managed to pass my last year of high school. Dad bullied my admission into university. He couldn't manage Oxford. The low grades of my last year of school and my lackluster interview saw to that. Instead, I went to NYU. Justin was uptown at Columbia. I dropped out after my freshman year.

A week later Dad had a stroke and I took over Castleton, Inc.

Looking back, I can see the beginning of the end. Two years ago we started being denied dig permits, investors dropped us, museums questioned the authenticity of our finds, I overextended on projects and lost millions of dollars. Until finally, our debts were called in, and it was discovered that a series of bad investments and using our personal property as collateral meant that Castleton, Inc. was bankrupt. Completely broke.

Last week, I lost our family estate, our New York apartment, my dad's condo in Naples. All our possessions were auctioned off to pay our debts. Everything was sold.

I have no home, no car, and six hundred, seventeen dollars and fourteen cents in my bank account.

Two days ago, the news came that my latest find was a forgery. I pulled the artifact out of the ground myself and guaranteed its authenticity. But it looks to everyone in the world that I tried to foist off a fake as one last grasping, dishonest bid to hang on to a crumbling career.

I'm not sure how in two years I ruined what took my father thirty years to build, but I did. My life was like a line of dominoes just waiting to fall down and that first dig permit denied was the flick that started the collapse. Or maybe it started before that. Ten years ago, when I hid in the bushes and didn't try to save Andrew or his uncle. Not even when the men dragged them away. Maybe it all started when I learned that I'm a coward. Because I sat frozen under those bushes for hours. Hours. I didn't come out until the sun rose and I heard my dad yelling my name.

"Where'd you go just now?" asks Justin.

I look up at him and try to smile, but can't. "I was just thinking," I say, "I once said that I'd be happiest living my life in a tent, dirty and exhausted from digging." I gesture around the cabin. "Just think, this is near to my nirvana."

Justin looks around the room and shakes his head. "I know you might not see it now, but I'm glad you lost Castleton."

I look at him sharply.

He shrugs. "It was an albatross around your neck. You can't tell me that in the years you've run it you've been happy."

"No one is happy in their job," I say.

"I am," he says. "I love my job. I just won a two-hundred-million-dollar settlement. It was invigorating. When's the last time you were invigorated?"

I pinch my lips together.

"I'll tell you when," he says. "The last time I saw you invigorated was right before you left to find the *Heart*."

I look away from him. "That's not fair."

"No," he says, "it's not fair that you're still holding on to it. Let it go. I think..." He pauses and I look up at him. "I think if Andrew were still alive, he'd want you to be happy. He'd want you to move on. It's time. Castleton, Inc. is gone, good riddance. You're free. You can have a fresh start. You can move on."

I feel dried out, brittle like a leaf in winter. I've felt that way for years. It took me a year after I lost Andrew to start living again. And I learned how to live again, but I never learned how to be alive. My heart is all dried out. Justin thinks better of me, he thinks I can bloom again.

He reaches into his suit pocket and pulls out a blue velvet jewelry box. I know what's inside it. A family heirloom, his great-grandmother's engagement ring—a two-karat pink diamond set in platinum: my engagement ring, if I accept his proposal.

"Justin," I say.

He shakes his head and sets the box on the tray table. "I'm not asking," he says. "I'm just leaving it here for you to consider. I care about you. I want to see you happy."

"But we've never dated. We've not..." We kissed, once at New Year's five years ago, and once at a charity gala three years ago when I wondered if maybe I could love twice in my lifetime. "I don't love you," I whisper. He deserves my honesty. He deserves more.

Justin nods, completely unruffled. "I know. Em, you know me. I'm not looking for love. I want a wife I respect, someone I love spending time with, who I can picture growing old with. You're my closest friend. I don't want messy love and outsized emotions. I'm a lawyer, I like logic. You don't want another grand flame either. I get it. But I want a marriage and someday kids. I think you do too. I wouldn't expect you to give anything you can't."

Like love.

I step to him and wrap him in a hug. I was so lucky the day he decided to be my friend. I lean my head on his chest.

"You'll think about it?" he asks.

My heart thuds painfully against my ribs. Could I marry Justin? Let go of Andrew? Is Justin right? Would Andrew want me to be happy? Would he want me to move on?

"Yes," I say, "I'll think about it."

3

———

Emma

"You're Emma Castleton."

I look up from the public computer at the Romeo Library. A young librarian in a cute dove gray 1950s-style belted dress gives me a bright smile.

"Umm, ye-es?" I say. I've only been in Romeo for one sleepless night and this is the first time I've ventured into town. Until this second I was one hundred percent certain no one knew me here.

The librarian, her nametag says Jessie, turns and waves at a group of older ladies sitting at a puzzle table. "I told them so," she says. She turns back to me. "I saw your picture in *National Geographic* years ago, and then again on the cover of..." She trails off and her cheeks turn bright red. She probably remembers the magazine cover she's thinking of. It had my picture and stamped across my face was the word *fake*.

"Um, so, you're staying in the old Van Cleeve hunting cabin. That place is a real pit," she says.

"How'd you know?" I ask, surprised and maybe a little unsettled at how well-informed she is. "I just got here yesterday."

She shrugs. "Small town. Everybody knew someone was at the cabin within five minutes of your arrival. First, Marsha at the grocery phoned Wanda"—she points to the older lady at the table in the horn-rimmed glasses—"and said the Van Cleeve boy was finally here. Marsha recognized him because apparently he looks just like his uncle did fifty years ago. Then Wanda told everyone at Bridge club, when she went to the retirement center. So then Erma told her niece Chloe. Chloe lives with her husband out near the Van Cleeve cabin, and Chloe said Nick was in a huff because there was a Lamborghini SUV parked out front—"

"That's Justin's car," I say.

She nods and continues, talking faster than almost anyone I've ever met. "And Nick made a point to mention to Chloe that if that Lamborghini belonged to anyone named Matt Smith, he'd march over there and kick them out of town. Which made Chloe laugh."

"Ah ha," I say, not really understanding anything she said.

"So everybody in town knew that the Van Cleeve boy was here and he'd brought a lady with him. The only mystery was the lady's identity. Which now, I've solved. I'm Jessie, by the way."

"Wow," I say, sort of awed by her directness and cheerfulness. I hold out my hand, "I'm Em."

She grins, then takes it and gives a firm shake. "Glad to meet you. You're here for a dig, aren't you?"

"Um, no?" I look at my internet browser. I have a tab open for my email, another on an archaeology journal and a third opened to world news. Nothing about digs. In fact, I was just planning on spending the next few weeks cleaning up the cabin and deciding if I could brave the business world and restart Castleton, Inc.—under a new name, of course. Justin may have been right. Castleton was an albatross around my neck, but I loved uncovering the hidden treasures of the past. It sings to me. It always has.

I close the browser and sign off the computer.

"That's weird," Jessie mutters.

"What's weird?"

Her eyebrows lower. "Well, Miss Erma said you were going to find the Lost Treasure of Romeo and also, you'll find and marry your soul mate. She said it'd be all wrapped up within the week. Two at most."

"What?" I say. My voice comes out louder than I expected.

"Shhh! Jeez, keep it down, you're in a library," one of the ladies at the puzzle table yells.

"Oh boo, Petunia," says Jessie, "you danced the hokey pokey in here last week. Your cell phone was blasting at full volume. So ridiculous."

Jessie turns back to me. "Anyway. When are you going to start looking for the treasure?"

I look at Jessie, then at the senior ladies working on a puzzle of a red barn and cow pasture, then I look at the moms and toddlers in the children's area. They all *look* normal. The lady yesterday in the grocery store seemed normal. And I think I saw this Chloe person and her husband drive by last night. They looked normal too. But I'm beginning to suspect that people in this town may be a little off.

"It was really nice meeting you," I say. I give a smile and a small wave. "I'll probably see you around."

Jessie gives me a confused look, then she starts to laugh.

"Oh, right. Wow. You think I'm crazy. You haven't heard about Romeo before, have you?"

I shrug. "Well, I mean, it's a small town, with hiking and wineries and boutiques and..." Okay, I hadn't heard of it until Justin told me about it a few days ago.

Jessie nods, like I'd confirmed what she suspected. "Okay, so I'll try to condense seventy-five years of Romeo town lore so you can understand what you've landed in. Follow me."

She walks to a glass-fronted cabinet across the library, unlocks it and pulls out a heavy book. She drops it on the table and it falls open to a page with a photograph of a wedding. "You're in Romeo, New York."

"Yes," I say. We agree on that.

"Official Town of Love, USA," she says.

I think I remember seeing that on the Welcome to Romeo sign at the edge of town.

"Over there is Miss Erma." Jessie points to a petite, fine-boned older woman in a red silk shawl sitting with the other ladies. "She has been predicting soul mates since 1948."

Jessie flips through the pages until she comes to the first photograph. The writing under the photograph gives the names of the bride and groom. The flower girl is Erma—she's small, young and in a lace dress.

"She's never been wrong." Jessie flips through the hundreds of pages. I watch as the pictures flash by. "She predicted my match. Two of my friends' matches. Heck, half this town. Once she sees your soul mate, that's it, there's no question." She snaps the book closed.

I watch as she puts the book away. Then, "I'm sorry. What exactly do you mean by soul mate?" There's an uncomfortable itchy sensation on my skin.

"Your soul mate. Your true love. Your one and only," says

Jessie. "The man you're destined to love and who will love you. Your other half."

My stomach sinks and I press my hand against it. I've only ever loved one man. I've never regained the ability to love another. I lost it when I lost him.

I wonder if this Erma really is a psychic and not some, well...fake. Maybe she saw Justin's proposal. Maybe he's right and I can move on. My skin feels tight and itchy.

"Can I speak with Miss Erma?" I ask.

"Sure. Of course," says Jessie.

She leads me across the library to the crowded puzzle table. The table is in front of a large bright window overlooking green grass, the river and a little arched footbridge. There are six ladies and one older man sitting around the unfinished puzzle.

"Miss Erma? This is Emma, the girl you pointed out. I told her about your vision and she was curious about it," says Jessie. "She's never heard of Romeo. Or of the Lost Treasure." Jessie's eyes brighten at the last. "I did my fourth grade social studies project on the Lost Treasure."

I smile at Jessie then focus on Miss Erma.

"Nice to meet you," I say. My tongue feels thick in my mouth. I don't know why I'm so unsettled. She can't actually have seen anything or predicted anything. I'm sure it's a misunderstanding.

"You too," Miss Erma says. She takes in my dirty, dust-covered jeans, my bleach-stained top, and my tangled hair wrapped in a blue bandana. I spent the morning cleaning and then walked into town for a break at the library. I didn't have cell reception or Wi-Fi at the cabin, so I figured when I got to town I'd text Justin that the night went okay and not to worry. Then I'd send my dad's live-in nurse an update. I hadn't expected to interact with people. If I had, I would've washed off at the water pump and changed my clothes.

"So, you're psychic?" I ask.

Miss Erma's mouth turns down and she shakes her head. "No, not at all," she says. She picks up a blue puzzle piece from the table and pops it into place. When she looks back up at me, I see something in her eyes that reminds me of an old woman I once met at a market in Cairo. She was nearly one hundred years old, and the look she gave me made me feel as if she saw past all the things on my outside and instead saw right into my heart. Miss Erma doesn't look like that woman, but she reminds me of her.

"Oh, snap Erma," says one of the ladies. "I've been looking for that piece."

"If you're not a psychic..." I say.

"I don't see the future," she says. She smiles and the wrinkles around her eyes crinkle. "I see the present. When you came in the library I saw you and your soul mate and the Lost Treasure." She draws a line through the air, tracing something from across the room and then lands with her finger pointing at me.

I shiver.

"Erma, you're freaking the girl out with your all-seeing act. Cut to the chase," this is from the lady that Jessie called Petunia.

Erma blows out a breath. "Fine. You're no fun, Petunia."

"I'm lots of fun," says Petunia.

Erma shakes her head and looks at me like I should agree with her. "Okay," she says. "Here's what I saw. You're going to look for the Lost Treasure of Romeo. When you find it, you'll also find your soul mate."

I nod. "Okay. Find treasure. Fine." Treasures I can do. I've found plenty of those. In fact, thinking about finding some mysterious artifact in this cute little town has me excited. It's the other bit that I'm not sure about.

"What's the name of her soul mate?" asks Jessie.

Erma shrugs and tosses aside a puzzle piece that doesn't fit.

"What does he look like then? What was he doing?" asks Jessie.

I lean forward. Do I believe her?

"She knows him," says Erma. She looks up at me and there's a hint of compassion in her eyes, like she knows more than she's letting on.

A chill settles over me.

"Is he blond, blue-eyed?" I ask. My voice sounds distant.

She shakes her head no.

"He's wealthy, as wealthy as a king. He owns skyscrapers, an island," Erma says.

One of the older ladies whistles.

Not Andrew. The thought flashes through my mind. Andrew never wanted money or prestige. Although it couldn't be Andrew. He's gone. Dead and gone.

I pull my gaze back up from the floor and look at Miss Erma.

"He has power and status," she says.

I don't want him. Whoever he is, I don't want him.

"He doesn't really sound like my cup of tea," I say. Plus, I don't know anyone that fits this description. I shrug. "Sorry. I'll still look for your treasure though if you like. I could research. Apply for a permit."

In fact, it'd let me do what I love, outside of the tarnish of Castleton, Inc. and the cloud of the past. A way to move on.

"I'll take him," says Petunia. "I'd love an island."

The lady next to her, she looks like her sister, smacks her on the back of her hand. "We'll stay out of this one," she says. "No interfering."

"Good idea," says Jessie.

I give Erma a smile. "Thanks for the welcome. I'm sure your

predictions have come true in the past, but I don't think it's likely this time."

"That's what they all say," mutters Wanda. She pushes up her horn-rimmed glasses.

Erma purses her lips and pats a completed chunk of puzzle into the barn. "Maybe so," she says. "Oh, well. Gals, we need to finish this puzzle. I'm headed to my niece's to see the baby in two hours."

Jessie looks at Erma like she's lost her mind.

"Oh, well? Ooo-kay," Jessie says. She turns to me, confusion on her face. Then she shrugs. "Well, anyway. It's lunchtime. Can I take you out for a welcome to Romeo lunch? I could invite some friends for you to meet. I'll bring some books, tell you all about the Lost Treasure, then show you to town hall for your permit or whatever you said you need."

I look back at the table. The ladies all seem engrossed in the puzzle. Me and my supposed soul mate are completely forgotten in favor of a barn puzzle.

"Well, alright," I say to Jessie. "Thank you. That's really nice of you."

Jessie starts to walk toward the exit and I turn to follow. But a stray thought makes me stop and turn back to Erma.

"I'm sorry," I say, "but did you happen to see what my um... soul mate, I guess...what he looks like?"

Erma looks up from the puzzle and gives me a wide smile.

"I did," she says.

"Okay." My throat goes dry.

Erma pauses, watches me.

"What does he look like?" I ask.

"Tall."

I nod. Okay. Tall.

"Thick, black hair," she says.

My heart stops for a moment, then with a hard lurch starts up again.

I can feel the soft memory of thick black hair running through my fingers.

I swallow and try to clear the lump in my throat. "That's it?" I ask.

She shakes her head no, then, "Eyes so dark, they're almost black."

The air rushes from my lungs, hard and painful.

A picture forms in my mind of a black-haired, brown-eyed boy. Now a man.

"He's sun-browned," she says.

I close my eyes, like doing so can block out the vision.

"Not possible," I whisper.

Andrew's dead. We had proof. He died. I would've torn the world apart if I believed otherwise.

Erma continues. "He has a crooked nose and a long scar over his eyebrow."

"Ooh, a pirate," says Petunia.

"Shush," says the lady next to her.

I open my eyes and try to focus on Erma. The room spins around me. Andrew's nose was straight, he didn't have scars. But it's been ten years, he might...he could...

"I...I..." I don't know what I'm trying to say. "Is he in Romeo?" I finally ask.

"Start digging for the Lost Treasure and he will be," Erma says.

I blink and the room stops spinning and comes into focus. All I have to do is start digging and Andrew, if it really is Andrew, will come back to me.

I know what I have to do.

Petunia laughs. "A treasure hunt and a soul mate. What could be better?"

4

Andrew

I lean back in my leather desk chair and give a wry smile. I'm ninety stories above the streets of Manhattan, in my office, and, some might say, on top of the world.

I own the building, this and a dozen others. In each one, I have an office on the top floor. When I made my first million dollars, I promised myself that from then on I'd always be able to see the sky. So far, I've kept that promise.

I spread my hands out on the wide mahogany desk and reach for the manila folder sitting in front of me. I've been delaying looking at it, but it's time.

I open it and slowly flip through. The neatly printed pages are a blur of black ink.

This is it.

Five years after clawing my way out of the jungle, five years of selling my soul for money and influence, I've finally brought down Castleton.

But surprisingly, there's no thrill of success, no satisfaction, no catharsis. In fact, there's a distinct lack of feeling about the whole thing. I always imagined the satisfaction or relief I would feel when I took away everything Emma and her father loved, but...it's not there.

I glance at the Castleton, Inc. bankruptcy filing, the sale of their homes, the auction of their heirlooms and possessions. I pause and linger over the article with Emma's image—the word *fake* stamped over her face.

Finally, feeling courses through me. I scowl, because I recognize the emotion. It's the same one I had in the mine when I dreamed of seeing the sun. The aching in the chest, the raw desire like you're trying to reach something outside of yourself but know that you can't.

The feeling is yearning.

Yearning for her.

I snap the file shut and throw it on my desk. The documents fly out of the folder and spread across the polished wood surface. Emma stares up at me from the photograph. I grit my teeth and quash the yearning.

The mahogany door to my office swings open and my partner, Dominic Sato, strolls in. I push the papers into the folder and then lean back in my leather chair.

"Dom," I say in greeting.

"Finished the auction," he says. He strolls over to the built-in mahogany bar and takes down a glass. "The Ming went for twenty-two million."

I shrug, I figured twenty-one and a half. It was an imperial Ming vase similar to another that recently sold for twenty-one at Sotheby's.

Dom opens the bar freezer, grabs a few cubes of ice and drops them in his glass. He looks up at the wall of glass shelves lined with single malts, gin and vodka, but doesn't reach for a bottle.

"It's on the second shelf," I say.

"Aha." Dom grabs the gin and splashes a healthy dose into his cup. He tops it off with tonic. Then he crosses the office and leans on the edge of my desk.

"Cheers," he says.

"Salut."

Dom swallows a mouthful of the gin and tonic. I lean back and look out the floor-to-ceiling windows of my office. Manhattan is spread out beneath me. I have one of the best views in the city. I can see the silver shine of the sun reflecting off the top of the Chrysler Building and the crisp blue sky above the shadowed streets.

"How was Singapore?" Dom asks.

"The same." I just flew back from Singapore this morning. Dominic and I own Suffolk Auction House, with locations in New York, London and Singapore. I met Dom in a bar in Cartagena, Colombia. I had a pocketful of gemstones and the burning desire to find and sell rare goods until I became so rich that I could make anything happen. Dom, a wealthy, entitled American, was bored and had the burning desire to prove to his family that he was more than a polo-playing second son. We both succeeded. The partnership works because, like my uncle said, I'm an artifact bloodhound. I have the uncanny ability to find priceless items. And Dom has the uncanny ability to put prices on priceless items and sell them for exorbitant amounts.

I haven't hunted artifacts since I was with Castleton. Instead, I go to estate sales, small auctions, markets in forgotten corners of the world, small villages lost to time, and the items seem to find me. Five-thousand-year-old vases, jewelry worn by queens, paintings by the masters—it's all out there, waiting to be found.

"So. Emma Castleton," Dom says.

I jerk, startled, then force myself to relax. I look at him and narrow my eyes. I've never mentioned Emma to him.

"Who?" I ask.

Dom smiles, strolls across the office to the windows and sets his glass on the sill. He looks down at the street and then up at the Chrysler Building. Dom has a habit of silence, thinking that if he waits long enough I'll speak. It works on other people, but never on me. Finally, Dom turns away from the view of the city.

"Seeing the world from up here sometimes makes me forget how we got our start," he says. He puts his hands in his pockets and leans against the glass. "I was on my way to the bottom, drinking myself through South America, and you, well, you were on your way to prison."

I lift a corner of my mouth. Dom likes to exaggerate. He calls it marketing, I call it bull.

"The day we met, outside that bar, you got drunk. It's the one and only time I've ever seen you drink."

"True." I realized the day after I met Dom, during a head-splitting hangover, that alcohol would easily prevent me from achieving my goals. The oblivion of drink was almost as appealing as revenge. So, I swore it off.

Dom continues, "And you told me about a girl named Emma, who had eyes like stars and freckles like the milky way."

My skin goes cold. Dom watches me. He's my friend and my partner and he's seen the way I've driven myself to get where I am. He never asked what drove me or what was in my past. I figured it didn't matter.

"There are plenty of girls named Emma," I say.

Dom's eyes flick down to the manila folder on my desk.

"Are there?" he asks.

I resist the urge to put the file away in a drawer and instead I stand and walk to the window. The carpet of the office is soft and thick under my feet. When the interior designers put together our headquarters, they wanted the offices to exude luxury. They succeeded. My office is the perfect example. The hand-crafted bar, the designer couches and antique mahogany desk, the Chihuly glass sculpture hanging from the ceiling, it all boldly declares that Suffolk Auction House is the epitome of refined luxury. The entry to the building has a thirty-foot modern art sculpture and a waterfall—it never fails to awe people and encourage them to part with millions at our auctions.

The lights of the chandelier reflect in the window. The sun has nearly set and my reflection looks back at me from the window. My image is indistinct and I don't look closely. I know what I'll see. A black haired, hard-eyed man, with no softness to him, wearing a twenty-thousand-dollar suit and a quarter-of-a-million-dollar watch. I see what everyone else sees: money and power. A man who has more.

My mouth twists.

I turn away from the image of myself. "I'm headed out," I say.

"I'm headed down too," Dom says.

I slip the file and my laptop into my briefcase. Dom doesn't say anything until we make it to the street. I turn north and walk up the crowded sidewalk. Business suit-clad people are heading toward the subways and hailing cabs. There's a line of thirty or so people waiting for their turn at a food cart. The heat of summer, the steam and musty smell from the subway grates, the smell of car fumes, food carts and hot pavement mix together to make the unique scent of New York. I used to wonder if I'd ever come across Emma. I'm in New York a few weeks every year. But then I realized, even if I did, she wouldn't recognize me. I look nothing like my eighteen-year-old self.

"I met Emma Castleton once. Years ago, at her debutante ball," Dom says casually.

I look at him from the side of my eyes and carefully keep from clenching my jaw. "Don't you live in Soho?" I ask. It's a rhetorical question. He does. He should be heading south, and I should be in the backseat of my Maybach, being driven back to my penthouse apartment.

But Dom wants to talk, and I'll listen.

"She came with Justin Van Cleeve. He and I went to school together. Still meet up to play tennis a few times a year."

I'm not surprised. Dom grew up in the circle of New York elite and knows all the best families. It's part of what makes him so good at what he does. I know most of them now too. In New York, London and Singapore. They accept me as one of their own.

I stop at the intersection and wait for the light. A crowd gathers around us, a great mass of people crowded together, waiting to cross.

"Do you remember what else you said at that bar?" Dom asks.

I look over at him. He stares straight ahead at the crossing light.

"No." I don't remember the conversation at all. Although I do remember bottles of rum and racing turtles and a handshake sealing our partnership.

The light changes and we move forward across the street with the mass of people. Taxis honk and people talk on cellphones or to each other. A jackhammer sounds in the distance. When I first got here the noise of the city was too much after the dark silence of the mine. I would retreat to the center of Central Park and pull in deep, gasping breaths, then I'd emerge onto the street again and push myself back into it.

We get to the sidewalk and Dom says, "You took your rum bottle, lifted it up and toasted, *'To Emma, the most heartless, coldest bitch in the world, someday I'll have enough money to satisfy even your greedy heart.'* Sound familiar?"

A prickling travels over my spine. "Not really. Doesn't sound like me."

"Agreed. You avoid women in favor of merciless business hours." Dom shrugs. "Frankly, I forgot the conversation. At least, until Van Cleeve mentioned the Castletons last month at tennis. He told me about how they'd been losing contracts, losing credibility, losing investments."

We turn down a side street to avoid another mass of people waiting for the light to change.

Dom continues, "Look, I'm all for destroying the competition. I've done my share of it, and enjoyed the hell out of it. Plus, Edward Castleton is a bona fide bastard. I can't say he didn't deserve a comeuppance."

"But," I say. I can hear the "but" in his voice. Dom has a softer heart than me. Hell, a rock has a softer heart than me.

"But nothing," he says.

We move into another crowd of people streaming out of an office building. A young boy zigzags through them, bumps into me and grips my jacket to steady himself. Before he can dart away I reach out and grab his arm.

"Hey!" he shouts. He's skinny and pale. He's wearing dirty shorts and a torn shirt and is probably about fourteen. And he's as slippery as a fish. I hold his arm tight.

"What's up?" asks Dom.

"Hand it over," I say.

The people walking by part around us. No one glances our way.

"Hand what over? Let go of me," says the boy. I have to hand it to him, he's got bravado.

I consider him for a second, then give his hidden pocket a

thwack. My wallet falls to the sidewalk—along with a watch, a small clutch and a billfold.

Dom lets out a low whistle.

I grab my wallet and put it back in my inner pocket.

"Hey mister, that other stuff is mine. You can't take it," says the boy, bold as they come.

"Is that so?" says Dom. "I'll call the police." He pulls out his phone, but I hold up my free hand and gesture for him to wait.

"What's your name?" I ask.

The boys eyes dart around and he nervously licks his lips. "Johnny," he says.

Which is a fake name. No doubt about it.

"Alright, Johnny," I say. "We'll be taking these other items to the police."

He scoffs but then goes silent.

"You need to stop stealing," I say. The boy gets an angry, mulish expression.

"Sure thing, Mr. Rolex, I'll do that real soon."

I don't know whether to laugh or shake him. "Listen to me. If you need money, come to Suffolk Auction House. Tell the security guard at the front desk, his name's Stefan, that I sent for you. I'll get you a job."

"Uh huh, right. Sure thing, mister."

Then, faster than I can respond, the boy twists his arm free, bends down, scoops up the items on the ground, and takes off down the sidewalk. It takes half a second.

I stare after him, then pat my pocket to make sure my wallet's still there.

Dom laughs and shakes his head. "You can't save all of them."

I watch as the boy disappears around the corner. "I know," I say.

"Do you?" he asks. "There's Henry and Ollie in London.

Lim and Aria in Singapore. The boy in Cairo, oh and who was it in Tangier?"

"Karim," I say. He was stealing to buy medicine for his mother. She isn't sick any longer thanks to a stay in a nice private hospital.

We start to walk again. I'm surprised to see we've walked a long rectangle and are nearly back to our building. We slow and then stop by the entrance. We're close enough that I can hear the sound of the waterfall when the door to the lobby opens as people exit.

"Right," Dom says. He puts his hands in his pockets and leans against the glass side of our building. The Suffolk Auction House sign is illuminated above him. "Look. I'm going to be straight with you. I don't know what grudge you have against Castleton, but I know you're in love with his daughter."

At his words I let out a surprised laugh. "Is that what you call it?"

Dom looks up at the darkening sky, brightened by the lights of the buildings.

"I met Van Cleeve for tennis yesterday. He told me Emma's in a little town Upstate called Romeo. That she's digging for some lost treasure. He thinks she'll clear her name. Make the name Castleton great again."

"Not likely," I say.

Dom shrugs, "Who's to say?"

A sudden spark of anticipation lights in me.

The dull, empty feeling I had earlier recedes.

It's not over yet. That's why I didn't feel satisfied. Because Emma's not ruined, she's not devastated. I still have more to do. For instance, I could find a lost treasure in a small town before Emma lays her hands on it.

"Did you know," I say, "I've been thinking about taking a

trip Upstate for quite some time. Maybe you can do without me for a week or two."

Dom nods. "I think I can do that."

"Good." My mind's whirring, thinking, planning, anticipating.

Can I do this? Should I? I glare down at the sidewalk. Of course I should. If I don't, what's been the point of any of this?

"One more thing Van Cleeve said."

"What's that?" I ask, distractedly.

"Van Cleeve said he proposed."

I look at Dom, "Proposed what?"

Dom shakes his head. "Marriage. He asked Emma to marry him."

The noise of traffic and the city streets fades, and there's a distant howling in my ears.

"Andrew? Did you hear me?"

I swallow and shake my head.

"She's getting married," he says.

The New York sky is dark and the city lights look like stars. Suddenly, I'm back in the tent with Emma.

"We'd be married?" I whisper to her. I brush my lips over her mouth.

She smiles at me. "Mhmm."

Then the scene morphs and I see her smiling at Van Cleeve, holding *The Heart.*

A taxi honks and I'm back in Manhattan, in the present. And the current me, the one who knows that the Emma of my dreams isn't the real Emma, knows exactly what to do. How to finally end this.

I'm headed to Romeo, to make Emma fall in love.

So I can break her heart.

5

EMMA

IT'S BEEN A FEW DAYS SINCE I ARRIVED IN ROMEO AND IT already feels like home. The cabin is clean, I have a new blanket and sheets for the bed, and it seems like I've met nearly every person that lives in the town. Jessie introduced me to her friends, Chloe, Veronica and Ferran. And then they introduced me to everyone else in Romeo as the legendary Emma Castleton, the woman who will find the Lost Treasure of Romeo and her soul mate in the same week. After that introduction, no one in town forgot my name or my face.

"Hi, Emma, did you find the treasure yet?" Mrs. Charles calls from outside the used bookstore.

I wave to her. "Not yet. Just got the permit to begin looking," I call across the street. It's a beautiful summer day and the brightly painted businesses along Main Street look cheery and welcoming in the sunshine.

Mrs. Charles waves an old book at me, then jogs across Main Street. I smile and wait for her.

"I'm glad I caught you," she says. She pushes her wind-tangled gray hair back behind her ears. "I found this in my local history section. It was written back in 1927. Do you think it'll help?" She holds out an old hardcover book. The cover is faded with black block lettering. It's entitled *The History of the Lost Treasure of Romeo, New York.*

I thumb through the brittle pages. They are yellowed, torn in many places, and the text is faded. But the book looks like a treasure trove of information.

"This is wonderful," I say.

Mrs. Charles beams, "Then keep it. No charge. Just be sure to invite me to your wedding. I love a good wedding." She looks at me expectantly.

"Oh, um...ah, of course...if it's in Romeo, or...uh, ever."

She pats my arm, "I'm looking forward to your news."

I frown as I watch her trot back to her bookstore. I'm not sure if by "news" she means finding the Lost Treasure or inviting her to my nonexistent wedding. I look down at the book and walk the rest of the way to the SweetStop.

When I get there, Jessie, Chloe and Veronica are already seated at an outdoor table. Jessie texted last night inviting me for a morning coffee.

"It's the weirdest thing," I say as I sit down. "Mrs. Charles just gave me a book in exchange for my assurance that I'll invite her to my wedding."

Veronica chokes on her coffee.

Chloe looks at me in surprise and then hits Veronica on the back.

"Thanks," gasps Veronica.

"You're getting married already?" asks Jessie. "Dang, you work fast. It's been what, two days since Erma's prediction?"

"Three—" I say.

Veronica coughs, then clears her throat. "I'm sorry. I thought you said you're getting married."

"No," I say. I hold up the old book. "Mrs. Charles gave me this book in exchange for a wedding invite in the future."

"Ooooh," says Chloe. "That makes sense."

They all nod to each other.

"Why does it make sense?" I ask.

"Veronica got married in Italy, and when Erma showed the pictures of the wedding to Mrs. Charles she was super envious," says Jessie.

"And by now, everyone in town has heard that your soul mate owns an island," says Chloe. She gives me a mischievous smile.

"So Mrs. Charles is probably envisioning the photo album she'll have from your island wedding," says Veronica.

I look down at the book, then back up at the girls. I wrinkle my nose. "First off," I say, "this random Richie Rich guy may be my soul mate, but that doesn't mean I have to marry him."

In fact, if he's not Andrew, somehow miraculously alive, I don't want anything to do with him.

"Exactly," Veronica says. She shoves a plate at me. "Have some donut holes."

"Thank you," I say. I grab one then pause with it halfway to my mouth. "And secondly, Erma didn't say what kind of island he owns. It could be a frozen island off the coast of Antarctica, or a barren rock a thousand miles from land. Island doesn't mean awesome. Just like soul mate doesn't mean true love."

Chloe makes a noise of disagreement.

But Veronica nods. "Exactly."

I pop the donut hole in my mouth. The cinnamon and sugar melts on my tongue and the cakey donut is still warm. It's so good.

"Come on, Vee. You're supposed to be a soul mate convert," Chloe says.

Veronica shrugs. "Maybe Emma isn't into finding her soul mate. Maybe she just wants to dig old stuff out of the ground for the rest of her life. It's her choice. Right?"

I nod and clear my throat. "Yeah," I say. "Exactly."

"So what did you learn about the treasure?" asks Jessie.

I flip open the book. At the front is a map of Romeo in 1927. "Pretty much what you already know," I say. I'd been doing research online and at the library. "In the eleventh century, a group of Vikings sailed over from Greenland and travelled inland. They settled here in the valley west of the mountain, near the Romeo River. The leader loved his wife desperately."

"Romeo's first soul mates," says Chloe.

"But she died, right?" asks Jessie.

"That's where the story gets fuzzy. Some accounts say she died, others say she went back to Greenland, still others say she got lost in the forest and never returned." I shrug. "Nobody knows."

"Sad," says Jessie.

Veronica nods and shoves a donut hole in her mouth.

I look down at the book. "After that, all the accounts agree. In his grief, the Viking husband built a stone treasure room for his wife, full of gold and jewels, necklaces, bracelets, and rings, hoping that the untold wealth would entice her to return to him."

"Wow," Jessie says.

Chloe turns to her, "You've heard this story before. Like a thousand times."

"It still gives me goose bumps."

Veronica nods and pushes the plate at Jessie. "Sugar."

I grin. Then I point at the old map in the book Mrs. Charles gave me. "From the research I've been doing, I think the treasure is near...here." I drop my finger to the map.

Veronica leans forward and looks at the page. "That's the meadow near the state forest, by the caves." A slow smile spreads over her face and she gets a faraway look in her eyes.

"My permit was approved," I say. "I'm going hunting." I smile as a happy anticipation fills me. Justin was right, I haven't felt invigorated since before *The Heart*. But I do now.

I look up as Ferran rushes up to the table.

"You won't believe it," she says. "Or you will, but I don't."

"What is it?" Jessie asks.

Ferran turns to me, "You remember I work at the Town Hall?"

I nod. She's the director of Romeo's tourism board, and from what Jessie said, she lives, eats and breathes her job.

"Well. I was standing at the copier when I heard the Parks team say another permit request came through for the Lost Treasure. Apparently, they approved it." She widens her eyes.

I swallow. I can hear my heart thudding in my ears. Everyone looks at me. I swallow again.

"Who is it for?" I ask.

Please say Andrew, I pray. Please say Andrew.

She shrugs. "I don't know. I just know Miss Erma was right. Your soul mate is coming."

My phone rings and I pull it out of my pocket. I'm walking back to the cabin from the bakery and haven't made it far enough out of town to lose reception.

It's Justin. "Hey," I say.

"How are you?" he asks, voice warm. I can hear midtown traffic in the background. He must've stepped out of his office.

I smile. "I'm good. I'm headed out in a bit to poke around the woods. See what I find." There's a trailhead near the cabin that leads up through the forest to the meadow I want to explore.

"You sound happy," Justin says. "Guess Romeo's agreeing with you. Maybe I'll come up next weekend, take in the sights."

I pause, a twinge of guilt pokes at me. "Justin?"

"What is it? You'd rather come down to the city?"

I stop walking and sit down on a mossy boulder near the edge of the country road. I take a breath, then, "Remember I told you about the ladies I met in the library?"

"Sure. They told you about the Viking settlement."

I rub my hand over the spongy moss then curl my fingers into a ball. "Right. Exactly. I'm sorry, but I didn't tell you everything they said."

He laughs. "Is this about my uncle? Yes, he was an old degenerate. But you know me, I'm nothing like him."

I look up at the blue summer sky. "It isn't that. There's this lady here, and everyone says she sees soul mates, and that she's never wrong, and she saw mine. My soul mate." I say it all in a rush and once it's out I slump down against the rock.

Justin is quiet. For ten seconds there's only the noise of midtown traffic and construction. Then he finally says, "I'm assuming from your tone of voice that this lady didn't say that I'm your soul mate. And also, that whatever she said, you believe her." He says this in a light voice that masks whatever he's feeling.

I blink up at that sky. "Yes. I mean, I know it sounds crazy, but yes, I could believe her. Maybe."

"Do you want to tell me about it?" he asks. Which is when I know Justin is the best friend I could have.

"She saw that I'd find the Lost Treasure, and she said when I start looking for it, my soul mate will come."

He sighs. "Anything else? Because, to be honest, that doesn't sound very credible. Scam artists read people and play on their emotions. Tell you what you want to hear."

I close my eyes. "I know."

"Did she say anything else?"

"That he's wealthy and powerful."

"Oh, so she was talking about me," he says, and I can hear the smile in his voice.

"He owns an island and skyscrapers."

He laughs, "Em, this sounds like a bad one-nine-hundred phone call with a two-bit psychic. What else, is he also a prince in disguise? A movie star? Come on. I'd blow this apart in court."

"Okay, yes. You're right. It is ridiculous. But everybody here believes it."

"And people also believed the earth was flat and that instead of migrating, birds spent winters sleeping underwater. Just because people believe it—"

"Doesn't make it true," I say.

"Exactly. If you like I can go buy my very own island today. My family already owns our building, so, we're set there. Done deal, I meet your psychic's soul mate vision."

I hold back a laugh. "Please, don't buy an island. Then you'd also have to dye your hair black and wear brown contacts."

"Really?" he says, and suddenly, his voice has sobered. "You think she's talking about Andrew."

I look down and kick my feet through the tall grass at the base of the boulder. "Would you hate me if I told you I desperately hope that she's talking about him?"

He pauses for a long moment, then, "No. I already knew it. But, Em, like I said. You need to let him go. It's not him. It's just a lady scamming an entire town. You know it's time to move on, this is just you, scared to do it."

"What if it is him though? What would you say if he showed up today? I know it's unlikely, but what if?"

He pulls in a long breath. "I'd say...that I'm happy for you. If he's the person you remember, if he's become the kind of man you deserve, a good man, Em, one that makes you happy and treats you right. Then I'll be the first to congratulate you."

"But?" I ask.

"But Andrew's dead. This lady is a scam artist playing on your past."

"Right," I say. Because there is a part of me that's been wondering since I heard Miss Erma's prediction, that if Andrew is alive, where has he been all these years? Why hasn't he contacted me? Which makes me think, it's not him after all. Andrew wouldn't ever let me believe he was dead for ten years while he was out making a fortune. He'd never do that. "So when some guy shows up claiming to own an island, I should tell him to get lost?"

"Unless that guy is me."

I laugh. "Do not buy an island."

"I'll come up in a week or two. If some random guy shows up in a suit, with black hair and brown eyes, you can bet the bank it's a scam."

"But the little old ladies were so sweet," I joke.

"Scam," he says.

I jump up from the boulder and trot back to the road. "What about finding the Lost Treasure?" I ask, jokingly. "Is that a scam too?"

"If there's a treasure, you'll find it," he says loyally. "If there isn't, you'll have had a nice break in the country before coming back to the city to build your new business."

"Thank you," I say. "For everything."

"I do have an ulterior motive."

"You want to pose with any Viking armor or weapons I find?"

"Exactly. I'll see you soon. Try not to drink any more of the Romeo soul mate Kool-Aid."

"You got it."

I smile and start walking up the dirt and gravel shoulder of the road. The cabin is only two miles away. A robin hops on the ground nearby, poking around for food. It's mid-summer, the weather is perfect, and I'm in the mood to go for a hike. I'll poke around the woods and see what I find.

Two hours later, I'm hiking on the trail near the meadow I pointed out on the map. I'm in old faded jeans, my hiking boots and a tank top. A drop of sweat slides down my chest. It's nearly noon, and even in the shaded forest, the day has moved from temperate to hot. I take a swig of water from my canteen then put it back in my day pack.

Before coming out, I skimmed the old hardback book that Mrs. Charles gave me and something caught my attention. The author claimed that the treasure room was in a large cavern near the settlement. He'd found a stone marker, now at the Romeo Historical Society, that seemed to suggest that the treasure was in a cavern. I'm going to swing by the Historical Society tomorrow to check it out.

I wipe at another drop of sweat and pause to take a moment to appreciate the lushness of the woods. It smells so clean and crisp, like new growth and soft breezes. There are wild raspberry bushes near the trail, and birds jump through the bramble, collecting the fruit. I let out a soft sigh. It's beautiful here.

The vibrant summer greenery of the forest climbs over

boulders and rocky outcroppings. I narrow my eyes. A few yards off the trail I see what looks like the opening to a cave. Veronica told me the other day at lunch that there's a huge network of cave systems in the area. She warned me, really adamantly, to be careful of them. I won't go in without proper precautions, but I want to see what it looks like.

I step off the trail. A stick snaps under my boot and the birds in the bush startle and fly away.

"Sorry," I call.

I step over a mossy log into the brush. Then, I hear a noise. A sort of snuffling growl. My skin prickles in that awareness that humans still have from thousands of years past when we were hunted by big predators. Something's behind me.

Slowly, I turn.

Oh no.

There are two black bear cubs less than ten feet away. But they aren't the problem.

My heart starts to pound. The problem is their mother. She lets out a growl and I know instinctively that she sees me as a threat.

I freeze.

"Back away slowly," a man says.

I nearly jump out of my skin. I swing my head toward his voice. He's in the woods to my right, farther from the bears, about twenty feet away.

I only catch a quick impression of a tall, wide-shouldered man before the mother bear growls again and I look back at her.

"Clap your hands and shout, make yourself look bigger," he says.

I try it. I clap my hands as hard as I can and shout, "Hey! Hey!"

The bear snuffs and shuffles toward me.

"Didn't work," I say to the man.

"It's okay. Keep your eyes on her, but move toward me," he says. His voice is tenor deep and raspy, and projects a calm strength. I'm sure I've never heard his voice before, but something about the cadence of his words makes my heart lurch.

The bear takes a step toward me. She's big, with thick black fur, a brown muzzle, and powerful arms that look like she could crush my head with one swat. She stands up on her hind legs and stares at me. She's over six feet tall, at least a foot taller than me.

I quickly look over at the man then back at the standing bear. He's cautiously moving toward me through the woodland growth and is now only about ten feet away.

"Don't worry, she's just getting a better look at you. She's not going to attack."

"Okay," I say. I lick my dry lips. Then take a careful step back. Then another. My ankle hits the log and I fall backwards over it. The bear drops to all fours with a loud huff. I scramble back up to my feet.

I take a second to glance over my shoulder at the man. He's only a few feet behind me. I get a quick impression. Six foot two or three. Expensive, tailored clothing. Thick black stubble, sunglasses, and a baseball hat. Dark tanned skin.

I don't know him.

The way he stands conveys the powerful, muscled confidence of a jungle cat. No wonder he's not afraid of the black bear.

I look at the mother bear again. She's watching us.

I take another step back and hit the warm muscled chest of my would-be rescuer. His hands reach up to my arms to steady me.

"Careful," he whispers.

His fingers softly press into my bare skin. I inhale sharply at the electric pulse that shoots through me when his fingers drift over my arms. Then I realize that his hands on my arms isn't the only place we're connected. My back presses against his warm, hard chest, and my butt presses into his thighs. I can feel the heat of him through my jeans and I have the sudden aching urge to lean into him.

A stranger. A random stranger I've never met.

My nipples go hard and brush against the soft fabric of my old tank top. I shiver.

"You okay?" he rasps. His fingers brush over my arms and goose bumps form.

"I'm okay," I say, but my voice sounds breathless to my ears.

"We'll back away together. Nice and slow."

I nod. He takes a small step back and I move with him. The bear tilts its head and studies us.

We take another step back. I can't see where we're going, I trust the man behind me to steer us right. When he moves, I move. He takes a step and I follow. I can feel his breath ruffling the hair coming out of my ponytail. I can feel the beating of his heart against my back. His thumb traces a small circle on the inside of my right arm and my heart skips a beat. Instinctively, I want to arch back into him. I don't. Instead, I take another step back.

"Doing good. Almost there," he says, approval laces his raspy voice.

Pleasure floods me.

What's happening? Is this man the soul mate Miss Erma predicted?

"Look," he says.

The bear stands on her hindquarters again and watches us. Then she drops down and turns away, steering her cubs back into the woods. I breathe a sigh of relief and sag into him.

"Thank you. Thank you so much. I've never seen a bear before...you pretty much saved my life," I say, only half-joking.

"You're welcome," he says, and there's a wry note in his voice. "You weren't really in too much danger. That bear was more afraid of you than you were of her."

"You think?" I try to look up at him. I only catch the twisting of his lips into a self-mocking smile.

Then he takes a step back and starts to pull away from me. I feel his footing slip. He swings around. I move with him. In backing away from the bear, neither of us noticed we were backing ourselves to the edge of a steep muddy slope. Suddenly, the eroding soil gives way beneath his feet. I grab his hand. Then the mud pulls us both down the hill. I let out a sharp, startled scream as I fall on my back, and we flip over each other, rolling down the grassy, muddy slope. Saplings thwack me as I roll past, and the breath is knocked out of me as I crash over a decomposing stump. I try to grab onto long grass and plants to stop my slide. But I'm moving too fast. I roll over the mud and slick grass. My stomach flips with me. It's like the worst, muddiest, bumpiest roller coaster ever. I manage to catch a fistful of grass and slow my tumble, but then the man slides into me and we're both rolling together again, a tangle of arms and legs.

Finally, we hit bottom. Not with a gradual slowing, but with a bone-jarring thud. I'm on my back in a pile of muddy leaves. They crackle beneath me. I try to pull in a breath, and my lungs fight it. Finally, I manage to drag a breath in, although it's hard with a solid, well-muscled man half-sprawled on top of me.

"Ouch," I say.

He groans, shifts his weight off of me, and lifts himself over me. Sometime during the fall his sunglasses and hat fell off.

He leans in and studies my face. His chest is so close to mine that when I breathe, my breasts brush against his shirt.

My head spins. I stare up at him. The sun filters through the trees and backlights him so he looks almost like an angel, glowing with golden light.

His face is less than six inches from mine and I feel the magnetic pull of him.

The forest is still spinning and I'm having a hard time focusing.

"You okay?" he asks.

I squint at him and try to catalogue what I'm seeing.

Tall.

Black hair.

Brown eyes so dark they almost look black.

Sun-dark skin.

A crooked nose broken too many times.

A raised white scar thin as a knife blade over his right eyebrow extending to his hairline.

He looks dangerous. Like a dangerous man. Like no one I've ever met.

I see all these parts, but I can't put them together, because none of it makes sense.

He's too tall, too wide, too hard, too intense, too...everything.

He's Andrew, but not.

I don't stop to think, I lift my hand and put it to the thick stubble covering his firm jaw. I run my fingers over the soft, prickly beginnings of a beard. He lets out a low growl. I feel it vibrate my fingers.

His eyes shift to my lips and he focuses on them like he's Odysseus returned to Ithaca. Like he's seeing his home, his love, for the first time in years.

"The sun," he whispers. I don't know what he means. I stroke his cheek at the ache in his voice.

He reaches down, his finger hovers over my lip and then he touches the freckle over my mouth. The one Andrew loved.

And that's when the pieces snap together and my brain finally lets me understand what my soul knew before I even saw his face.

My heart slams against my ribs, aching to get out and go to him.

"Andrew?" I whisper, fear in my voice. Because what if it isn't him? "You're alive?"

His shoulders stiffen and his gaze flicks up to mine. The soft, yearning leaves his eyes and they shift to match the man with the long scar, the hard mouth and the crooked nose. But then, as quickly as they went hard, they soften again.

He lets out a silky laugh. "What do you think, Emma? Don't I look alive?"

It's like a bolt of lightning hits me. I launch myself at him. He falls over and I roll on top of him. I hold myself to him and touch him everywhere. His arms, his shoulders, his abdomen, his face. His face goes blurry and I realize it's because I'm crying.

"Andrew," I say, and I repeat it over and over again, like a prayer that's been answered.

Finally, minutes later, my hands slow, and I notice that he's completely still, that he's been watching me like the jungle cat I imagined. He hasn't touched me back, or said my name, or done anything at all but watch me. I stop and pull back from him. A twinge of trepidation rises and I push it down. This is Andrew. My Andrew.

He stands and offers a hand to pull me up. I take it. His hand is warm and calloused in mine. He lifts me to my feet. The dry leaves crumple under my boots. I look down and realize I'm covered in mud, leaves and burrs. My jeans are torn and my tank top is so old it's almost see-through. In contrast, he looks unruffled and at ease. He's in an outfit that I know from my last trip to the SoHo boutiques, costs thousands of dollars, and there's a watch on his wrist that costs as much as a house. He gives me another half-smile, one I never saw from him in the past. He only used to give me full-blown grins. Wild and carefree.

The thought returns again.

He's Andrew, but not.

What happened to him?

"What is it?" he asks.

"I have a question," I say.

He gives a quick nod.

I look at him, then, "Do you own an island?"

He gives me an assessing look, but doesn't answer.

"And skyscrapers?"

He tilts his head like the jungle cat I imagined him to be. Then he nods an affirmative.

Shock washes away the pleasure. He's wealthy, powerful, owns an island, and he let me think he was dead and gone for ten years.

The question is, why?

6

———

ANDREW

"HOLD STILL," EMMA SAYS.

She brushes the blood from a small cut on my forehead with a soapy washcloth. She doesn't have to tell me to hold still. I wouldn't be able to move even if her cabin were on fire. She's touching me for the first time in ten years and I realize that in all my scenarios playing out her destruction, I missed the most important variable.

The fact that I can't resist her. Even knowing she's deceitful and manipulative, I still want her. The feeling burns inside me. My hands shake with the urge to grab her and drop her to the floor so that I can taste her everywhere and make endless love to her. I clench my fists to keep from reaching out to touch her.

I concentrate on the sting of the soap in the cut and let it clear my head. I'm sitting in the only chair in Emma's cabin, an old recliner facing a decades-old television. Nearby, there's a lumpy bed on the floor. I swallow and tear my gaze from the rumpled sheets.

"Thank you for the first-aid," I say. I lift the right side of my mouth in a smile. After coming out of the mine, I had to practice smiles that didn't terrify people or have them run in terror from business deals. This one worked best, although Dom claims I still look like the devil when I give it. Apparently it doesn't reach my eyes.

"Of course," she says. Her fingers shake as she cautiously smooths antibacterial ointment into my skin. I had a first-aid kit in the glove compartment of my Land Rover. I'd parked on the fire road in a meadow, only a quarter of a mile from the trail. After Emma and I climbed up the hill I drove us back to her cabin.

Emma fumbles with a bandage. Her hands shake as she tries to open the packaging. She keeps sending me nervous, assessing glances. I'm not a fool, I caught the fear in her voice when she realized who I was. She's terrified that I know what she's done.

The crazy thing is, being near her makes me not care anymore. She makes me forget my uncle, the years of torture, the dark. She makes me forget my promise of revenge. Right now, the only thing I care about is making her mine.

I need to change my strategy. It's what's helped me be so successful all these years. I adapt when new information comes in. The fact is, I'm not going to be able to function until I sink inside her. I can't think with wanting her so badly.

Emma reaches up and smooths the band-aid over the cut on my forehead.

"There. You're all fixed," she says.

Right. If only it were that easy.

She looks up at me through her eyelashes and I see the gold flecks in her hazel eyes that always reminded me of the stars.

"Thank you," I say. I stand, and when I do I accidentally bump the tray table next to the recliner. The table wobbles and a small velvet box slides off it and bounces to the floor.

"Oh," she cries.

I bend down and grab the box. It's clearly a ring box. I rub the velvet of the container. When I look at Emma her eyes are wide, worried, and she's biting her lip.

Ah. It's an engagement ring. From Van Cleeve.

I have an almost irresistible urge to throw the ring into some dark, undiscovered hole where no one will ever find it.

I relax my shoulders and keep what I'm feeling off my face.

"Sorry," I say. I hold out the box to her.

A red blush rises on her cheeks as she reaches for it. Our fingers brush as she takes it. I don't miss the irony of me handing Emma another man's engagement ring. She puts the box in her pocket and then turns her face to the side, away from me.

Looking at the ring in her pocket I make a decision. There's no way in hell I'm going to let her marry another man. She's mine. Mine to make love to. Mine to destroy.

But if I want to make love to her then I need to woo her.

"Have dinner with me," I say.

She looks back at me. The line between her brows crinkles in thought. I swallow the lump in my throat, I want her to say yes so badly.

"What is it?" I ask.

"Andrew," she says.

I nod.

"Where have you been?"

I can't tell if it's a trick of the light or if there are actually tears in her eyes.

If I didn't know better I'd almost believe that she has no idea what happened to me.

"That's a long story," I say.

"It's been ten years. Why didn't you find me? You could have written. Called. Anything. Why didn't..." She swipes at her cheeks and turns away. "What happened to you?"

My heart beats hard against my ribs like my fists against the walls of the mine. I shrug and give my nonchalant half-smile. "After the men attacked the camp my uncle and I met up with a man named Crudell. We went into business together." In a manner of speaking.

I watch Emma carefully. When I say Crudell's name she stiffens and her eyes fly up to mine.

"But—" She cuts off. Her eyebrows draw down and she shakes her head.

My muscles go tight and an icy rage washes through me. I saw the checks with her signature, confirmed with private investigators that Emma and her father had communicated with Crudell for years, but still, apparently some part of me had hoped she wouldn't know who Crudell was.

"What?" I ask, keeping my voice light and relaxed.

"We hired a man named Crudell to find you." She tilts her head to the side. "I paid him an annual fee to search for you. To notify me if he ever..."

I shake my head, then shrug, as if it's of no importance. As if the fact that she betrayed me to a psychopath is completely irrelevant.

"He's been dead five years now."

"Oh," she says. "That's when we received news that you were truly gone."

I'll bet.

"I wanted to contact you," I say.

She looks up at me as if she wants to believe me more than anything in the world.

"But I couldn't. If I could've come sooner, I would have. I

would've moved heaven and earth to reach you." Once upon a time that was true. "Do you trust me?" I ask. I reach out and brush a finger over the freckles on her face.

She shivers and then leans into my hand. She looks at my face, the long scar over my eyebrow. The one received on my sixth escape attempt. Finally, she nods. "Yes," she says. "I trust you."

Cool satisfaction spreads through me.

"Let me take you to dinner," I say.

She shakes her head no and I hide a flinch.

"Why not?" I ask. "There was a time when you wanted to eat every meal with me."

"I have too many questions." Then she shrugs. "And I'll probably cry a lot. And want to touch you."

At her confession my body aches to be touched. Suddenly, all I can think of is her hands on me.

"We can go to my place. I'll make you dinner. Like I used to," I offer.

At that, she smiles. "You still cook?"

I nod. "For you, I still cook."

One of the advantages of wealth that I never realized as an eighteen-year-old nomad was that money makes things happen. Within two hours of notifying my assistant that I'd be heading to Romeo for a few weeks, he had my Land Rover ready, my bags packed, and a house rented in Romeo and stocked with all my favorite foods and drinks.

The house is a regal stone mansion near downtown that was built by one of the founders of Romeo. It has all the modern conveniences, but still has the original woodwork, the plaster walls, and brass and crystal chandeliers in many of the rooms. There are built-ins, window seats throughout, and wood burning fireplaces in many of the rooms. The walls are creamy white, the woodwork is dark cherry, and the furniture is antique. The original glass windowpanes from the eighteen hundreds are in many of the rooms and it gives the house a soft wavy dreamlike glow. I explored the house before heading out to the forest and so I know exactly where to lead Emma.

"Here's the kitchen." I flip on the lights and watch Emma as she takes in the room. The kitchen is bright and cheery with plenty of windows, a breakfast nook and a long marble island with upholstered stools facing the prep area.

"You can sit while I make us dinner." I brush a hand over the air near her back, not quite touching her. She changed her outfit and washed off at the water pump while I waited in the Land Rover. She's wearing a pair of shorts that look like they were once jeans and a loose light blue tank top that dips and shows me a hint of the space between her breasts every time she leans forward. She braided her hair and put on lip gloss, but that's it. She looks nothing like the sophisticated socialite I saw in the magazines, and everything like the Emma I once spent my summers with. I wonder if she did it on purpose. If she's playing to our shared history.

Or perhaps she really is completely bankrupt and this outfit is the best she has left.

I look down at myself and shake my head. Our situations have completely reversed.

I pull out a stool for her to sit in. She shakes her head.

"I'd rather help."

"Ah." I push the stool back in. "You didn't know how to cook before."

"I've changed too," she says.

Don't I know it.

"Can I get something out of the way?" she asks. She clasps

her hands together in front of her and her knuckles go white. I look away from them and back up to her face.

A trickle of trepidation flows through me. "Of course."

"I...you make me nervous. You're like the Andrew I knew, but..."

"Different?" I give her my half-smile.

She swallows and nods. Her eyes flick to the scar on my forehead. "I've dreamed of you coming back to me for so long. But I realize I never thought about what happened after I threw myself in your arms. For instance, what did we talk about, what did we do, where did we go? My dreams always ended with you reappearing. I never thought about the fact that time would have passed and that we'd both be different people."

She glances at my clothing, my watch, at the kitchen around us.

"I don't know if you're even the same person I remember. That scares me."

"I'm not," I say.

She looks up at me and her eyes widen.

The person I was is dead.

"Oh." She lets out a breath and looks down.

I step forward and reach out, gently touch her clasped hands. She breathes in quickly and looks up at me.

"But maybe you can come to love the new me," I say. There's a battle waging inside me, between tenderness and revenge. I lift my hand from hers and reach out to push back the hair falling across her forehead. It's the exact color I remember— autumn wheat burnished by the golden sun.

Her lips tremble into a smile. She steps forward and I'm taken by surprise when she wraps her arms around me and drops her head to my chest.

I carefully put my arms around her. Her lips brush over my shirt in a ghost of a kiss and I go hard in a millisecond.

"Remember what you asked me, that last night?" I ask.

She grips my shirt and bunches it into her fists. "About becoming partner?"

"Not that."

"About Oxford?"

"Not that either."

Her hands grip my shirt tighter and she moves closer to me.

"If you'd ever thought about making love," she whispers.

I nod. "Every day. For the past ten years."

She stiffens and I hold still, waiting to see what she'll do. She doesn't move, doesn't leave my arms. Finally, she relaxes into me. I run my fingers over the base of her spine.

"Did you know this is the Official Town of Love, USA?" she says. Her voice is muffled by my shirt.

"Really?"

She nods. "There's a lady here who predicts soul mates. A few days ago she told me you were coming. She said you're mine. My soul mate."

For a second, I stop breathing. "Is that so?"

"Apparently, she's never wrong. She's predicted hundreds of matches."

"Interesting."

I'm speaking in single-word sentences, but my mind is a blur. Either Emma believes we're soul mates or she's playing another game. Either way, it leads right into what I want. Emma, in my bed.

"Do you believe her?" I ask.

Emma pulls back and steps out of my arms. "I didn't at first, because I thought you were dead. But now I do. Does that scare you?"

"Nothing scares me."

She gives me a look. "Everyone's afraid of something."

"I'm not," I say. You're only afraid if you have something to lose. "Except...missing dinner."

She gives a short laugh and I move into the kitchen. I open the refrigerator. It's stocked with fresh produce, cheese, sauces, milk, and meat.

"How about prosciutto-wrapped chicken and a salad?"

"Even your taste in food has changed. I'd be happy with beans and rice. That's what we would've had if we stayed at the cabin." She smiles at me and I look again at the outfit she's wearing. It's not a scheme. The reports I received were dead-on. She's beyond broke.

I did that to her.

Except, she doesn't seem unhappy.

I pull the ingredients from the refrigerator and place them on the island countertop. "Well, tonight we're celebrating. We can go big."

She rolls her eyes and grabs the vegetables. "I'll make the salad."

I start prepping chicken.

We stand side by side at the counter and work on dinner, as if we've been doing this together for the last decade. It's completely domestic and so normal. I imagine that this could've been our life if we'd taken a different course.

"Tell me about you," I say.

"Me?"

"Yes. You. You keep telling me I'm different, but I imagine you're different too. Did you go to Oxford, take over the family business?"

I already know the answers, no and yes. But I'd like to hear her take on the past. I pull out a cutting board and start slicing the meat.

Emma stands at the sink and runs water over a strainer, washing the lettuce. She swirls the lettuce around, stalling.

"No," she finally says. "Gosh, it's hard to remember you missed everything."

I push the cut meat aside and start on the next chicken breast. "What happened?"

"I wasn't well," she says.

I glance up at her and she gives a small smile and shrugs.

"I thought my..." She pauses, then, "I thought the man I loved was dead. It took me almost a year to come out of...to be able to...interact with people again."

I look at her, my brows drawn. That doesn't fit with what I know. "Then what?" I ask.

She shrugs and sets the lettuce aside and starts washing the tomatoes. "Then I nearly didn't graduate from high school. Dad had to bully my acceptance to a college in New York. I failed that too. I couldn't..."

She stops and sets the tomatoes aside. "Nothing mattered anymore. So, I dropped out of college after my first year."

I stare at her, try to see her expression, but her head is bowed.

"What about your plans? What about *The Heart*? You could've dominated the field with that discovery." Which she and her father did. I've seen the articles.

She lets out a low laugh. "My dad demanded I attend the gala where we donated it. That was the night I considered...I seriously considered ending my life."

I step toward her involuntarily.

She looks up and her eyes are filled with gold stars. "It seems stupid, doesn't it, knowing you're alive."

Is she telling the truth? Looking at her, I find that I...believe her. "I'll be grateful forever that you didn't." I can't imagine what I would've done to come out of the mine and find her dead. Even though I hated her, I still wanted her alive.

"You can thank Justin," she says.

"Who?" I ask. Even though I know. My jaw clenches at the thought of him.

She smiles, "Justin Van Cleeve. He's my best friend."

I wait for her to say what else he is to her, but she doesn't. "And then what happened?"

"My dad had been handing off business tasks to me, he wanted me to take a more active role. I didn't want to. But then he had a stroke and I had to take over the business whether I wanted to or not."

"You were in charge of everything for the past, what, seven, eight years?"

"Eight."

She sets the vegetables on a cutting board and starts to cut them. The only sound for a moment is the knife hitting the cutting board methodically.

I turn back to my cutting board and start wrapping the prosciutto around the chicken.

"How is your father?" I ask, keeping my voice light.

"As good as you'd expect. He's had multiple strokes now. He has to have a full-time nurse with him, he's pretty weak, he doesn't communicate as well, he gets upset easily. I don't think life turned out quite the way he expected, and neither did I, so I guess that frustrates him sometimes."

I give her a rueful smile, "I bet."

I put the chicken into an oiled pan on the stove while Emma tosses the salad into a bowl.

I'm starting to get an uncomfortable feeling that I missed something about Emma, that I missed a piece of the puzzle that once inserted, completely changes the entire picture. I turn back to her.

"So, is running Castleton, Inc like you'd imagined it to be?" I ask.

She shakes her head. "I don't run it anymore. I lost it." She looks at the expression on my face and shrugs. "Don't look so upset. It's not your fault."

I wipe my face of any emotion. There's a guilty gnawing feeling in my gut. It is my fault. I orchestrated everything.

"Apparently, I'm not a very good CEO. I made bad investments, tarnished our reputation, somehow I rubbed officials the wrong way," she continues. "I loved hunting for artifacts, you know me. But the other stuff...I could take it or leave it. You were right. When you said you didn't want more, or to chase prestige, you were right. It's not what it's cracked up to be. I have nothing now, I lost it all, but when I did, I felt lighter than I have in years."

I wonder if that had anything to do with a proposal from Van Cleeve. Except, she's admitted she thinks we're soul mates. Which, I would guess, means that she's going to turn Van Cleeve down.

A warm satisfaction grows in me.

"So, you're happy?" I ask.

"Happier than I've been in years."

She looks at me from across the kitchen and I'm pulled into her gaze. We stand for five seconds, ten, just looking at each other. The air is thick with want.

Finally, she clears her throat and looks away.

I pull the chicken off the stove and place it in the oven. It'll be done in a few minutes. I move to the cupboards and pull out plates and salad bowls.

Emma moves to grab silverware and napkins.

"Tell me about you," says Emma. "I gave you the Cliff notes version of my life. What about you?"

I set the plates and bowls on the counter and pull out wine glasses. I saw a Pinot Grigio in the wine cooler that'll pair with the chicken and prosciutto.

I'm stalling. I'm hesitant to answer Emma's questions.

Nothing makes sense. It's hard to think, being so close to her and not touching her. But also, what she's saying doesn't match with what I thought I knew. The private investigators I hired to look into Emma and her father confirmed that the money they paid Crudell came from their private bank account. Emma signed checks to Crudell for five years straight. The investigators also found evidence that Castleton and Crudell had met years earlier at a charity gala at the natural history museum in Chicago. The more I dug into their past, the more I learned that Castleton had either bribed or bullied his way through every country and every find of his career. Emma had seemed complicit, it was her signature on the checks after all.

Except.

"You've got the dark and mysterious down," Emma says. She scoops salad into the bowls. "I'm not very mysterious. What you see is what you get." She smiles and gestures at herself.

Is that true?

"Who hired Crudell?" I ask.

"What?"

"Crudell. Tell me about him."

The oven beeps and I pull out the chicken. I bring it back to the counter then grab the bottle of wine and a corkscrew. Emma watches as I serve the chicken then pour the wine.

Her eyebrows pinch together. Then, "It looks delicious. Thank you."

"Of course." I lift my wine glass and hold it up to her. She lifts hers. "To reunions." I touch my glass to hers and the wine splashes back and forth, letting out a subtle fruity fragrance.

"To finding each other," she says.

I drink a sip of wine and watch the line of her neck as the wine slides down her throat. I take another drink to hold back a groan.

"So. Tell me," I say.

She sighs and sets down her glass. "My father hired him. I first spoke to him on the phone a week after we returned to New York. My dad said he was an old family friend that lived in Colombia and that he had many contacts and specialized in..." She looks up at me, and her brows lower. "In kidnappings."

My mouth is dry and I feel a cold sweat breaking out over me.

"That wasn't true," I say.

"Obviously," she says bitterly. "Since you went into business together. I have years of correspondence with him. Begging him for a scrap of information about you. Every email, he claimed to be close, or to have found a new lead, but then later he'd say it was a false lead. He strung me along for years."

"You paid him?"

"One hundred thousand dollars a year."

She looks at me and her eyes flash. "Did you use that money to fund your business. Whatever it is you do?"

My entire body has gone cold.

"Do you have the emails?"

"What?"

"The emails from Crudell, do you still have them?" My voice comes out harsh, harsher then I intended. Emma scoots back.

"I...ah...yes?"

I swallow and rein in the swirling maelstrom inside. "Can I see them?"

She nods. "Okay." She takes out her cellphone and opens her email. I watch as she opens a folder labeled A.S. My heart lurches with recognition. They're my former initials, Andrew Santiago. She doesn't know that's not my name anymore.

Inside the folder is five years' worth of emails. "May I?"

She nods and hands me her phone. I take it and start to

read. My stomach rolls. I feel sick. Laid out in front of me are Emma's desperate pleas for answers, waning hope, and Crudell's carefully constructed lies. After ten minutes of reading I set the phone down on the counter. Our food has gone cold. But I wouldn't be able to eat anything anyway.

She searched for me. She was desperate to find me. She...

"My word."

She presses her lips together and twists her napkin in her lap. "It's kind of funny, isn't it? Since you were never really lost."

"Emma," I say and my voice breaks on her name. I reach forward and place my hands to her cheek, run my fingers over her skin. "You tried to find me."

The world that I've been living in for nearly a decade turns upside down and the final piece that I've been missing falls into place. She didn't know. She wasn't a part of this. She tried to find me.

"Of course I did," she cries. "Do you know what kind of hell it was thinking I'd hidden like a coward while you were taken away and killed? I was a coward and you and your uncle suffered for it. Wait. Rigo. Is he okay too?"

I shake my head no.

Emma drops her head into my hand and presses her lips to my palm. "I'm so sorry. I should've tried harder. I should've come out, come after you."

"No. I told you to stay there. I wanted you to."

A small smile crosses her face. "Yes, but when did I ever do what you told me to? I shouldn't have started then."

I brush my hand through her hair and drag my thumb over the smoothness of her jaw. She makes a low sound in her throat. The sound lights me on fire. I pull in a harsh breath.

My word.

She didn't know.

She didn't know.

There's only one answer then. It was her father, and her father alone. I make a quick decision. Emma can't know. She loves him, she always has. Learning what he's done would hurt her too much. The past can stay in the past. According to Emma, Castleton has had multiple strokes and he's not functioning well. He isn't a danger to anyone anymore. My chest tightens. I can leave it. I can let everything rest, leave the past in the past. I look at Emma. Her bright eyes and her freckles. If I leave the past alone, we can have a life together. All I have to do is bury the past and never dig it up. She doesn't have to know what her father did, and she doesn't have to know what I did to take revenge on him.

From this moment on, we start over.

I brush my thumb over her lower lip. "I didn't go into business with Crudell."

"What do you mean?"

"He was with the men who attacked the camp. He murdered my uncle and forced me and others to work for him in his mining operation. I was his...prisoner...for five years. Until he died, and I escaped. You and your father were fooled. Taken in by a sadistic scam artist. He must have targeted you." The lie slips out easily. Let the past rest.

"What? No." She jumps off her stool and reaches for me. She pulls me to her and rubs her hands over my arms and my back. She pulls me to her and I let her. "I didn't know. How dare he! I wish I knew where he was buried, so I could dig him up and kill him again."

She has a bloodthirsty look on her face, one of angry retribution, and I imagine her as an avenging Boudica, leading an army against the Romans after her husband's death.

"After I escaped," I begin, then I pause.

She looks up at me. "Yes?"

"I wasn't right. I wasn't in a good place. It took me another five years to come back to you. I'm sorry. I'm very sorry." I say it for not coming back to her, and for everything else too.

She puts her hand to my chest. "I would've waited another five years. However long you needed."

A warm happiness seeps through me and filters into all the dark places that haven't seen light in a decade. I stand and pull her against me. She fits. She fits me perfectly.

"Emma."

"Yes?"

"I'm going to carry you upstairs, tie you to a bed so you can't get away, and make love to you all night long until your voice is hoarse from screaming my name. If you don't want that, then you need to walk out the front door right now. Understand?"

She backs away from me, out of my arms. I watch her chest rise and fall as she takes in a shuddering breath.

I hold still, waiting for her assent, even though every instinct in me is telling me to take her upstairs and claim her as mine.

She reaches over to her dinner plate and shoves a piece of prosciutto covered chicken in her mouth, then another. She makes an appreciative sound. Then she takes a long gulp of wine.

What the hell?

She pops a tomato in her mouth.

"What are you doing?" I ask, although it comes out more as a groan.

She looks at me and a slow grin spreads across her face. "I figure, if I'm going to be kept up all night, then I'll need my strength."

She eats another piece of chicken and then licks the juices from her finger.

Holy hell.

"Is that a yes?" I ask. Please say that's a yes.

She takes a drink of wine and then sets the glass onto the marble counter.

"Emma?" I say, my patience nearly gone.

She runs to me and I catch her in my arms. "Yes," she says. "Yes. Yes. A thousand yesses, yes."

A small laugh comes out of me, and I'm surprised by it, because I haven't truly laughed since the last time I was with Emma.

I hold her up and pull her against my chest. She's still a lightweight at five foot two, and I'm two inches taller and twenty pounds bulkier than the last time she saw me. But we still fit.

"Well? What are you waiting for?" she asks. "I've been wanting you to do this since you fell on top of me at the bottom of the hill."

7

———————

Emma

"Emma."

I open my eyes wide at the rough growl in Andrew's voice. His eyes are lit with a wild yearning that makes the muscles deep inside me clench in response. I wrap my legs tighter around him and press myself against him. I let out a small needy noise when his hard length rubs against me.

Whatever he sees on my face makes his eyes blaze hotter.

"Yes." I dig my fingers into his shoulders and rock myself into him.

He drags in a deep breath. It looks as if he's fighting a battle with himself, between taking me upstairs and making slow, sweet love, or taking me right here, right now.

"Right here. Right now," I say.

Whatever restraint was holding him back breaks. He comes unleashed. His mouth crashes over mine. I cry out at the contact, and when I do he swoops in. His tongue licks me, tastes me, owns me. Every time his tongue darts in, the deeper parts of me shoot pulses of pleasure in response. I hear small whimpering noises and I realize it's me. One of his hands grabs my lower back and pins me against his length. His other hand cups the back of my head and holds my mouth to his. It's as if he's terrified that if he lets me go, I'll disappear.

I know exactly how he feels.

I grip his shoulders, then draw my hands over his arms and his chest. I tug at his shirt and try to pull it up over his head. He pulls his mouth away from mine and lunges toward the kitchen wall. My back hits the cool plaster. Andrew grabs my hips and wedges me between his length and the wall. He grinds his hips against mine and I rock into him. I'm aching for him. Each time he presses into me I cry out. I feel drunk on him. My body is an electric current that pulses in every spot he touches. I need him everywhere, to touch me everywhere.

I'm finding it hard to think, to articulate what I need, so instead I rub myself against him. "P...p...please."

I tug at my shorts. My hands tremble and my legs shake as I work at the button, then the zipper. I can't manage to pull off my shorts while Andrew holds me up. I whimper.

"Hell," he swears.

He lowers my feet to the ground and I shove down my shorts. He looks at my pink panties and I see the hunger in his expression. It's the look of a starving man presented with a Christmas feast. I yank off my tank top and stand before him in my bra and panties.

His hands tremble, then he clasps them into fists. He's holding himself back. But I don't want him to. I've waited ten years for this and I don't want him to practice restraint. I unsnap my bra and drop it to the ground. My breasts are heavy and they tingle when the cold air rushes over them. My nipples harden as his eyes land on them. His chest heaves as he lets out a harsh exhale. I'm hot and achy and I need him. I push my panties down and stand before him naked.

For a second, he doesn't move. His eyes are stunned. Completely thunderstruck.

I smile at him.

He looks at my mouth and then swoops down to kiss me.

"You've undone me," he whispers against my mouth. "I'm undone."

Then, he grasps my hips and lifts me up. I hit the wall. I rub my bare breasts over his shirt. When my nipples drag over the fabric, they send a mirroring spark between my legs. I grab at the fly of his jeans and yank them open. His length springs free. He's holding me by my hips and his fingers dig into my thighs. His entire body is tense with wanting. I look down at the evidence of just how much he wants me. I close my hand over him and he lets out a hiss that sounds like he's in pain. I watch his face as I rub my hand over him. He clenches his jaw and his eyes go unfocused. I pull my hand down. He's silky smooth, as hard as iron, and hot. The heat of him soaks into me. I gently squeeze his length and he jerks in my hand. He tenses even more, holding still under me. As if he's afraid to move.

So, I move for him.

I lift my hips and guide the tip of him to my entrance.

I'm wet and throbbing, and when the heat of his tip touches me, all my insides clench.

"Emma. My word." He grabs my mouth with his and sends his tongue in. One hand holds my hips and the other grabs my braid. He kisses me as he rocks against my opening. Never quite going in, only teasing.

I hold his length in my hand, the tip of him barely inside me. I pull myself free of his kiss and try to lower myself onto him. He closes his eyes and grits his teeth. Sweat trails down his forehead.

"Please. I need you."

That's all it takes. Andrew opens his eyes. He captures my gaze, holds my eyes with his stare. And thrusts inside me.

The world explodes. It takes one hard thrust of his length inside me and I'm convulsing around him. I cry out and he shoves himself in deeper, harder. He gives a raw-throated cry and buries himself in me. I spasm around him again. I can feel it through my entire being. As if my whole body is throbbing around him. His eyes go black with heat and need and I try to collapse against him, but he holds me up. He thrusts again. *My word.*

"I've missed you. I've missed you so much." There's such an aching need in his voice. "I've missed you." He goes still. "So much."

I whimper and rock on him.

I close my eyes and feel the heat of him. Feel where we're joined. I feel whole. With him inside me, I feel whole again. "I've missed you too."

With my eyes closed, I memorize the feel of him inside me. Then I start to move on him.

"Look at me," he growls. He holds my face in his hands. I open my eyes. His eyes are locked on mine. He thrusts. I toss my head, riding the wave of him moving inside me. "Look at me."

I latch onto the anchor of his eyes and ride the cresting pleasure.

"I'm yours, Emma. Look at me. I'm yours."

I cry out. He presses deeper inside me. Claims every inch of me as his own.

"I'm yours," he says, and he keeps saying it in time to his thrusts.

"I'm yours," I promise back.

The world spins around me. He's wedged into me so deep

that I can't tell where he ends and I begin. That's not right—there is no ending, no beginning.

"I'm yours," I say. "You're mine."

He shouts out and I feel him get thicker inside me. He shoves deeper, hits me so deep that I convulse around him again. His thrusts become faster, desperate, uncontrolled. He throbs inside me, fills me.

"You're mine...you're mine." He buries himself deeper and I cling to him. He stays buried inside me, slowly rocking back and forth. He kisses the edge of my mouth, my jaw, my earlobe.

I wrap my arms around him and drop my head to his shoulder. I take in a deep, shuddering breath. My thundering heart starts to slow.

I want to wrap myself against him, stay with him inside me for the rest of forever. I never want this to end.

I love him. I always have and I always will.

8

ANDREW

FOR THE SECOND TIME IN MY LIFE, MY WORLD HAS CHANGED
drastically in less than twenty-four hours. I'm still deep inside
Emma and I don't want to pull out. Ever. She's mine. I brush
another kiss to the corner of her mouth.

Never in my life have I experienced so much pleasure. I
never even imagined so much pleasure existed. There was a
moment when it felt like the universe stopped expanding, and
Emma and I stood still at its center. She's right, she's always
been my other half.

For this moment right here, I'd spend another dozen years
trapped in the mines. Knowing this was on the other side of
hell, I'd brave it again a thousand times over. Emma wraps
herself around me and leans her head on my shoulder. I kiss
her silky hair and breathe in her scent. She still smells like
forest leaves, fresh water, and mint. That's the smell of

innocence and love. I shift inside her and realize that I'm ready again. I want her, need her, that much.

"I'm taking you upstairs," I say.

She nuzzles my neck and I feel her smile against my skin.

I take the stairs two at a time and drop her on the four-poster bed in the master suite. She stretches out on the plush red comforter and gives me a heated look from beneath her eyelashes.

"So, this is where you tie me up?"

She looks around the room. The decorating fits the grandiose style of the old mansion. The four-poster canopy bed is dark wood with a wine red comforter and sheets. There's a chaise lounge and an antique armoire. Heavy velvet curtains are tied back with gold drapery cords. There's a stone fireplace with a thick wood mantle and a French impressionist landscape on the wall. On the nightstand next to the bed is a fruit basket, a bottle of wine, a corkscrew and glasses. My suitcase sits on a luggage rack near the armoire. The armoire has a mirror on the door. I look at myself. My face is hard. Even now. My jaw is dark with stubble and my eyes glint. One might say that I don't look any different than the devil that came out of the mine promising revenge. Except my clothing is wrinkled, my hair sticks straight up, and the edges of my lips curve upward ever so slightly. I'm a new man.

"Do you want to be tied up?" I give a small smile.

Emma looks at the tall wooden beams of the four poster bed. Then she nods yes. A bright red blush covers her from her pink breasts to her cheeks.

I let out a surprised huff. Then I walk over to the curtains and pull the gold tassel cords free. I yank the curtains shut, leaving the room as dark as fallen dusk. At the edge of the bed I slip out of my shoes and socks.

I lean over and switch on the soft yellow light of the bronze and glass table lamp. A small circle of light wicks away the night. I breathe a little easier. I haven't slept in a completely black room in five years, and even tonight, I can't face the darkness.

Emma reaches over and fingers my shirt. She starts to pull it up, over my head, but I stay her hand.

"Not yet."

"But I haven't seen all of you." The line between her brow wrinkles as she looks at me still in my clothes.

An uncomfortable feeling moves over me and I roll my shoulders and push the feeling aside. I walk to my suitcase and pull out a silk tie. "You don't need to see me for what I have in mind." I keep my voice light and teasing.

Then, just in case she decides to argue, I gently push her back to the bed. "Lay down."

She settles back into the down comforter. I breathe out in relief. I'm not quite ready to let her see me. Not yet. I'm also not ready to face the dark. Apparently, I haven't completely left the past behind.

I take the silk tie and wrap it over her eyes so that she's blind to me.

"Can you see anything?"

"No. Nothing."

"Good." I place a kiss on her lips, lingering over the taste of her.

Her hands alight on my shirt and she pulls it up. I let her guide it over my head, then toss it onto the floor. Her fingers brush against my chest. They feel like fire against my bare skin and I suck in a painful breath. I move her hands to my jeans and let her pull them down over my legs. Her fingers drag over my skin and I groan at the painful heat rising from her touch. I kick my jeans to the floor.

"Let me touch you," she whispers.

I take her hand, kiss each finger, then the center of her palm. Then I put her hand to my heart. It's one of the few places on my body not covered in a web of thin white scars. My back, my shoulders, my legs, all of it was cut into with a knife. Most of the scars are courtesy of escape attempt number twelve. Some are from the sharp, stabbing rocks of the darkened mine.

Emma presses her palm into my chest and then slowly trails her hand down my abdomen. My heart beat quickens as her hand moves lower. Finally, she grasps my length in her hand.

I groan as she holds me tight. She strokes my length once, then again. Then she bends down and places a kiss on my tip.

My length jerks in her hand and I nearly drop her to the bed and bury myself inside her again.

Instead, I pull her up and kiss her mouth.

"My turn," I say.

I take her left wrist and run my thumb over the underside. I place a kiss on her pulse, then I tie a loose knot around her wrist and secure it to the bedpost.

I trail my mouth along her arm, over her chest and then up her other arm, until I reach her right wrist. I secure it to the opposite post.

I work my way down her body. Touching her, drifting my hands over her, kissing her soft skin. I lick her breasts and she arches her back, offering them up to me. Then I work my way down the dip of her stomach, her lush thighs, her calves, all the way to her ankles. I kiss the inside of her ankle and tie another knot around her. I secure it to the bottom bedpost. Then I lift her other leg, drag my fingers along the inside of her calf, and kiss her there. I tie her final leg and knot it to the bedpost. When I'm done I look at her spread out beneath me. Her arms are open, her breasts are laid out before me, her legs are spread wide with her completely open to me.

She's panting. Her chest rises and falls in rapid, needy breaths. She looks like a gift from heaven, and she's offering herself to me. Completely and without reservation.

A wild, possessive need sweeps through me. One that urges me to claim her, again and again.

"Andrew," she whispers.

"I'm here."

And then I begin my onslaught. I touch her in all her sensitive places. I drag my fingers up her calves to the inside of her thighs. She raises her hips. I move on to her breasts. I lick them and suck them, I drag them between my teeth until she cries out for more. I move up to her neck, where I find her pulse point, and I wrap my lips around her and suck. She bucks up, so I lay my body across hers. Feel the heat of her under me. My length throbs against her, aching to be back inside. I run my fingers through her hair and pull her braid free.

I push into her and she lifts her hips again. "Andrew," she cries. She strains against the arm restraints. "I need to touch you."

"Not yet."

"I need to see you."

I move down, trailing kisses over her stomach.

"Not yet."

She lifts her hips again and lets out a low cry.

"Trust me?"

She lifts her hips again. "Yes."

I place my mouth over her swollen clit and suck. She lets out a sob and bucks against me. I hold her hips in place and run my tongue over her. Then I send a finger inside her. She's wet and tight and hot. I move my tongue over her and taste her pleasure. Every cry, every lift of her hips sends a jolt of happiness through me.

"Andrew!" she shouts, and her voice is hoarse with pleasure.

I pull hard on her clit and she convulses around my finger. I keep licking her, drinking in her pleasure until her spasms fade and she collapses back to the bed.

I look down at her. Her skin is flushed pink, it sheens with sweat, she has red marks on her thighs from my stubble, and there's the beginning of a purple love bite on her neck. She's so beautiful my heart could burst.

And because she can't see me and can't touch me, I let my face relax and reveal how much I would give up for her. How much I love her.

"I'm going to love you now," I whisper.

Then I lay over her and slowly push inside her.

When I do, my chest expands and I feel like I'm coming alive again. Coming into the light.

Inch by excruciating inch I settle myself inside her until I'm fully buried.

She gasps and I swear. I didn't imagine it when I made love to her in the kitchen. When I'm inside her, it feels like I'm in the center of the universe, touching the sun. I'm burning up from the heat of her.

I pull out and groan as her slick walls clench me. I can't think. I only know I need to be inside her again. So I start a rhythm, bury myself in her, find the sun. Pull out to the darkness. Plunge in her again and see the light. Until finally, even when I pull out, I'm so connected to her that the light's always there.

"Please," she cries.

When I try to pull out, she lifts her hips, keeping me inside her. She tightens down on me again and I feel the beginnings of another orgasm. She's clenching around me, tighter and tighter. Until I feel the cum moving up my length, aching to fill her. She clamps down on me and I shout out. Stars burst in my vision until the room is full of bright white light.

I roar as she convulses around me. A cataclysm of pleasure engulfs me as I pour myself into her. Everything I have. Everything I am.

The room is bathed in light.

I collapse to the bed and stay buried deep inside her.

Finally, my heart slows and the room fades back to semi-darkness.

"My word."

"Thank you," she whispers and I see a tear slide from beneath the silk tie.

"Shhh."

I reach down and untie her ankles, then her wrists. Before she can pull the tie free from her eyes, I pull the blankets over us. Then I turn her into my chest and wrap my arms around her. She lifts the tie free and tosses it aside.

When she looks up at me, her eyes are luminous and I can see the golden stars there.

"Don't ever leave me again," she says.

I kiss her brow. "I won't. I promise."

It's not me that I'm worried about leaving. She has more reason to leave than I do. I shift her closer.

"Tell me more about this soul mate prediction."

She makes a happy sound and wiggles her backside into me.

"There's a lady in town. Apparently, she's predicted hundreds of soul mates. She's never wrong. She told me my soul mate would come to me if I started looking for the Lost Treasure. I prayed it was you. Even though I didn't think it could come true, I prayed it would."

I stroke my fingers through Emma's hair and think about what she said. "What does she mean 'soul mate'?"

"You know. That one person in the world who makes you feel as if you've finally come home. Like after a lifetime of darkness, there's light in the world again."

My heart stops then starts again at her words.

"A soul mate is your perfect match. The solution to your Gordian knot."

I smile at her ancient Greek history reference. She's describing exactly how I feel about her. I press another kiss into her hair.

"You think that's you and me?"

She looks back at me. "Who else?"

I think of the engagement ring back at her cabin. "There's no one else?"

"No." She looks into my eyes and the hazel bleeds into the gold. "I love you."

A sharp jolt hits me in the chest and for a moment I can't breathe. By the look on her face I know she's waiting for me to say it back. And I want to. With everything in me, I want to.

But I can't.

She didn't tell me about the ring. She lied by omission.

I can't tell her about the dark, or my scars. Or her father's role in my abduction.

Suddenly, I can see that although we're lying naked together, there's a chasm between us.

The words "I love you" are stuck in the darkness inside me. Unable to reach the light.

There's a deep-seated fear stopping me from laying myself completely bare.

"I love you," she says again.

I squeeze her to me. "I know."

A heaviness settles over me and for some reason, a

foreboding too. Like the feeling I had when I held *The Heart* in the cave.

"Tomorrow we'll look for the Lost Treasure together. Just like old times."

"That sounds perfect," Emma says, but there's a hint of sadness in her voice.

"Let's go to sleep."

"Should I get the light?"

I shake my head. "No. Leave it on."

9

———

EMMA

THE ROMEO HISTORICAL SOCIETY IS IN A THREE-STORY rectangular building with large arched windows and tall columns. It sits just off the town square. It's built from the local sandstone, beige with hints of pink when the sun hits it just right. It's one of the original buildings and has a cornerstone with the date 1804 carved in it. According to the bronze plaque at the front, the building has a long history and has been the town hall, the court house, a library, a church, a movie theatre, and for the past fifty years, the home of the Historical Society.

Andrew and I were at the front door at eight-thirty on the dot. Just like the old days, Andrew can't stay in bed past five in the morning. He always said life was too exciting to sleep it away.

When I woke up at six-thirty, he was already dressed in jeans and a long shirt.

He was on the bed next to me with his laptop open. When

he saw me awake he smiled, kissed me more awake and then fed me the breakfast he'd made.

At eight thirty, a small, curvy woman with short blonde hair ran up to the front door and let us in. She'd gotten Andrew's email and would love to show us the Romeo runestone. Her name was Charlotte and she was the archivist at the Historical Society.

So here we are. It's not yet nine, and we have the runestone to ourselves. Charlotte left us after a few minutes to open up the rooms and check her email. Andrew and I are in the basement—from what I can tell it acts as a storage room of sorts. There are boxes, books, mannequins in clothing from the last two centuries, and enough documents to make any history buff drool. The fluorescent lights flicker and buzz and the air smells like old parchment. The Romeo runestone is in the center of the room. It's made of sandstone, it's about three foot high and two foot wide, and it has runic writing carved in the surface.

I look down at the weathered sandstone and try to decipher the runes. But it's nearly impossible to concentrate. Every time I start to translate, Andrew leans in and brushes his hand over the back of my neck. It's a featherlight touch, barely there. But his fingers on my neck remind me of the fourth time we made love last night. We went down to the kitchen for a midnight snack. Before eating, he bent me over the kitchen table, held me down with his hand clutching the back of my neck and entered me from behind. So now, every time he brushes his fingers over my neck, my body goes all tingly and my mind goes blank.

The back of his fingers drift over my neck and I shiver.

"What do you think?" he asks. He looks at the stone while his fingers play over my sensitive skin.

Concentrate.

"It's pretty incredible. There's so little evidence of Viking settlements in North America. I'm surprised this hasn't made its way through the archaeology circuit."

It's only in recent years that archeologists have found settlements using satellite imagery to scan for houses and farms covered by a thousand years of soil. Romeo, New York is farther south and west than anything they've found yet.

"In my experience, a lot of important findings are buried in museum basements and people's attics. They can stay hidden for hundreds of years until someone comes along and uncovers them. My guess is they don't realize what a treasure they have."

I think about the Ming vase I heard that recently sold at auction for more than twenty million dollars. It was found by a collector at a bed and breakfast. The owners were using it as a door stop.

Then I look over my shoulder at Andrew. He's studying the runestone with lowered brows. When he worked with my dad he had a better grasp of ancient writing systems than any of us. He'd rather read hieroglyphics than any high school textbook I shared with him. He used to make me laugh so hard when he read ancient graffiti carved into temples, tombs and monuments. No matter the era, people love to write *I was here*, or *Publius is stupid*, or *Philomena has big tits* on the walls. Now we do it on bathroom stalls, back then, they did it on pyramids and standing stones. But Andrew could always read it all.

I smile. "Do you remember when we visited the barrow?"

It was an old Stone Age burial mound that my dad discovered.

"The one with the obscene graffiti?"

I grin. "Mhmm."

I was fourteen and the graffitied sexual exploits of Thorni Longaxe fascinated me. The mound had been discovered by Vikings, and they weren't shy about carving into the walls.

They liked buxom widows, having sex, their weapons, treasure, and their dogs. Andrew and I went in late one night with a lantern and he whispered the phrases to me. It was the beginning of my awareness of him as someone more than a friend.

When one man claimed in runic graffiti that his dog was the most beautiful woman on earth we both ended up laughing until we cried.

Andrew raises an eyebrow. "Why do you ask? Are you thinking of trying one of Longaxe's positions?"

"No. Well…maybe later." I cover my mouth and hold back a snort at the surprise in his eyes, then the flood of heat in them.

"Is that so?"

I shake my head and pull my hand away from my mouth. "I just meant, you used to know futhark. Can you still read it?"

Futhark is the runic writing system used from about the third century to the sixteenth century by the peoples of northern Europe, Scandinavia and Iceland. There are sixteen letters in the alphabet, they're angular and written from right to left.

"Some. I'm rusty. I worked with a team in Denmark a few years back." He gestures at the runestone. "It reminds me of the Jelling stones."

The Jelling stones are massive runestones in Denmark from the tenth century. The oldest stone was raised by King Grom as a memorial for his beloved wife.

I nod. "Me too."

But then I turn back and look up at him. He just casually mentioned working with a team in Denmark and it gives me a hint to the years I missed. He hasn't said anything since yesterday about the five years that he was free but didn't come back to me. I wonder if he'll tell me about them or if it's too painful.

I set my hand on his forearm. "Is that what you did? Find artifacts? Did you work with archeologists the last few years?"

He tilts his head to the side like he's considering how to answer.

Maybe he won't answer. He's holding a lot back. My chest pinches when I remember him not saying I love you back.

He does. I know he does.

But.

The Andrew I remember never held back. Not in conversation, not in the way he moved or the way he lived. Everything was done with gusto. This new Andrew, he's more careful.

"It's okay. You don't have to answer. We have plenty of time." I smile at him.

He lets out a sigh, maybe one of relief.

"I was in Denmark too. Two years ago. Imagine, we might've run into each other."

He shakes his head no. That's right. He wasn't in a good place then. He wasn't ready.

I take my hand off his arm.

He lifts one side of his mouth in a half-smile that doesn't reach his eyes. "I can answer your question. I did still work in the field. I found out that you were right. I have an uncanny talent for finding artifacts and lost treasure. Honestly, I don't think I have the skill to do anything else. This is it for me." He holds out his hands and shrugs.

I smile at him, but for some reason what he's saying makes my chest ache.

"Maybe this is the beginning, then, of the partnership we talked about all those years ago. Once I get back on my feet and find the capital, I'm going to start a business again..."

I trail off because he has a strange look in his eyes.

"What? You don't have to go into business with me. I wasn't..."

He doesn't let me finish. He leans down and places a kiss on my mouth. I sink into him and wrap my hands around his neck. Suddenly, he pulls away and sets me back. I blink at the speed that he pulled away.

He turns away from me, toward the stone.

"Andrew?"

He shakes his head. "I'm trying not to take you on the floor next to a runestone."

"Oh. Ohhh."

I stay quiet while the fluorescent lights buzz and Andrew's breathing slows. There's a small smile on my face that I can't contain. When Andrew turns back to me his eyes are needy and heated but he doesn't look like he's about to strip me naked.

"So...futhark?"

He looks at me and shakes his head in obvious amusement. Then, "Right. I'm paraphrasing a rough translation here."

"Got it."

He steps forward and leans over the stone. He runs his fingers over the runes from right to left. "The stone says, 'Eric the Old, King of Vinland...there's some more titles there... ordered this monument made in honor of Vinland's Adornment, beloved wife, Thelgi. That she who won for herself his heart may find his treasure. It lies at Sol's...'"

"Sol, the Norse sun goddess?"

"That's right. It says, at Sol's barrow."

"Another burial mound?"

"No. That's not right." He frowns. "Let me think."

I stare at the rune. I'm not able to decipher it. Then I remember the book Mrs. Charles gave me. "There's an old book

I have on the Lost Treasure. The author seemed to think the treasure is in a cave."

Andrew starts to nod. "Right. You're right. It says cavern."

A thrill of excitement runs through me. "Okay. Sol's cavern. What's next?"

"That's about it. There's just one more line. It says…"

He stops and his shoulders stiffen. I step closer. His fingers hover over the last line.

"What is it?"

He shakes his head and visibly relaxes. "Nothing. It's not a clue. It says, 'Come back to me, my sun.'"

On the last line his voice comes out lower, rougher, and I shiver. I think of the moment he landed on top of me in the woods, when he looked down at me and said, "The sun."

I look at his expression, but he seems to have shrugged off whatever came over him.

"Should we go?" I ask. I've taken pictures of the stone and we now have more to go on. "We can plan our next move."

Andrew's eyes light up and he motions for me to precede him up the stairs. I wait for his hand to touch my back or linger on my neck, but he doesn't reach out for me again.

10

I'M IN SERIOUS NEED OF COFFEE SO WE DECIDE TO SWING BY THE SweetStop Bakery. The bakery is a short walk from the Historical Society, through a little open park and a rose garden in full summer bloom.

"Look at this. It's incredible." I point at the rose garden. It's about half an acre and is surrounded by a white picket fence covered in purple clematis and flowering vines. A white wooden trellis with climbing red roses is at the entrance. A stone path leads through the garden to the exit into the grassy park and then on to Main Street. Andrew and I walk through the trellis and I breathe in the rich old fragrance of dozens of antique roses.

"Wow. It's beautiful."

I look at Andrew to see what he thinks, but he isn't looking at the roses, he's looking at me.

"What?" I give him a self-conscious smile. "Don't you like roses?"

He tears his eyes away from my mouth and looks around the garden. There are at least fifty different varieties, each with a metal label in the ground nearby telling their common and Latin name. Maybe there's an agricultural school or a club that cares for this garden. Some of the roses are delicate with soft, small, pale petals and frothy yellow centers. Others are robust and showy in vibrant deep reds. There are fat bushes, delicate miniatures, and long-stemmed roses. Yellow, peach, white, crimson and pink. I reach out and touch the deep red petal of a rose hanging from the trellis. The petal is thick and velvety.

I look at Andrew again. The petal is nearly as soft as he was. His eyes go dark when he sees the expression on my face.

"I could learn to like them."

I smile and pull him along the little stone path.

"I love roses."

"Really? I didn't know that."

I nod. A bee buzzes by and lands on a pale peach rose.

"I always have. My mom grew them at our family home." A bit of sadness tugs at me. It's bittersweet and smells like roses. "When our house was foreclosed on...those roses were the only thing I...they were the only thing it was hard to let go of. I can't see roses without thinking of her."

I look up at Andrew. His jaw is tight and his eyes are dark and unreadable. "I'm sorry."

I shake my head. "It's not your fault. It was stupid of me to hang on to them. They aren't her. I put too much meaning in them."

He reaches down and takes my hand. His fingers stroke over mine. I lean into him for a moment, then start walking along the path again.

"Anyway. The reason I like them is because they're exactly how I feel about life."

He stops and turns me toward him. We're at the center of the garden near a sweet little fountain.

"How's that?"

I look up at him. I never noticed this before, but his lower lip has the same curving lushness of a petal. It's a juxtaposition against the hardness of his jaw, the harsh line of his cheekbones, his crooked nose and the long white scar over his eyebrow.

"It's just…" I lick my lips at the expression on his face. "I just mean, roses can hurt and make you bleed, they're almost guaranteed to hurt you."

"True."

"They're also beautiful. You see? Some people want the beauty without the pain. But life doesn't work that way, does it?"

He reaches up and brushes his thumb over my lip. Then, he gives me a smile. "I see what you mean."

I shrug. "Come on. Coffee calls."

We walk down Main Street, past the brightly colored shops and their window boxes overflowing with flowers. At the SweetStop my cellphone vibrates.

I pull it out of my pocket. "It's my dad. Do you mind?"

Andrew tenses. I wouldn't have noticed, but I'm still holding his hand, and for a split second his whole arm goes tight. Then he relaxes.

"No. Go ahead. I'll get the coffee." He gives me a smile, but it doesn't reach his eyes. I frown after him as he strides into the bakery.

"Hi Dad." I answer.

"Emma."

"I'm glad you called. Did Linda give you my update?" Linda

is his full-time nurse. After multiple strokes, he's become much weaker physically and has a harder time regulating his emotions and speech.

"She did. Come back to New York, Emma. You need to start Castleton again. Accept Justin's offer. Stop moping."

Wow. That was a whole lot to take in. I stare over Main Street at the bright buildings. I wanted to tell him about Andrew in person, but I think now is as good a time as any.

"Dad. Andrew's here."

There's silence on the other end of the line.

"Dad? Did you hear me? Andrew's back. He's come back. He wasn't dead. Crudell lied. It was some sort of horrible scheme. Andrew's back and, Dad, I love him. I'm not going to start Castleton again. I don't know what I'm going to do, but whatever it is I'm going to do it with Andrew." I'm speaking quickly and excitedly. I pause to take a breath and realize my dad still hasn't said anything.

"Dad?"

There's a wheezing noise coming from the other end.

"Are you okay?"

He starts to cough, and I wait for nearly a minute while he coughs and wheezes into the phone. Finally, he goes quiet.

"Okay, Dad?"

"Emma. Stay away from him." His voice is slightly garbled and he sounds extremely upset.

I shake my head. He must not understand.

"Dad. I'm talking about Andrew Santiago. Our Andrew."

"Listen." He harshly exhales.

I stop. A large cloud passes over the sun, dousing the warmth. I shiver.

"Whatever he says is a lie. Stay away from him. He's dangerous. He's—" My dad starts wheezing again. After his first stroke he had a really hard time regulating his emotions. I haven't seen him this frustrated since those first weeks all those years ago. He coughs and then yanks in a loud, phlegmy breath.

My heart beats hard, and I feel slightly ill. I don't know what he's thinking, but he's scaring me.

"Dad. I'm sorry I upset you. I'll talk to you when I'm back. It's okay. It's just Andrew. He worked with you for years. You know him. He's not—"

"Emma. Stay away—"

He starts to cough again.

My chest feels tight and my stomach rolls.

"Emma? Are you still there?" It's Linda, my dad's nurse.

"Oh, thank goodness. Linda, he's really upset. I don't know why. Can you...?"

"It's fine. I'll take care of it. I'll send you an update later today."

I let out a long breath. "Okay. Thank you. Sorry. It's been really stressful for all of us lately."

I let Linda go. And then I sit down at one of the metal café tables. I stare out at the painted brick storefronts but don't really see them.

I don't understand...

Why was my dad so upset?

"Here you go. I got you the Sumatran if that's—" Andrew comes out of the bakery, then stops. I look up at him. His shoulders are stiff and he has a wary expression. "What did he say?" His voice is flat, and my internal alarm bells go off.

I swallow down a lump in my throat. "He...he wasn't himself."

Andrew nods and carefully sets down two cups of coffee. His movements are quick and economical, and I notice that there are lines of tension around his mouth.

"Did something happen?" He sits down stiffly in the chair next to me.

I nod. The lump in my throat is back. "It was weird." I watch his expression carefully. "He told me to stay away from you. That you're a liar. And dangerous."

If I weren't watching so carefully, I wouldn't notice Andrew's eyes shutter. But I am. And I do.

"What is it? Tell me."

"Emma."

I stand and push back from the table. "No. Don't. What did he mean?"

His face pales and he closes his eyes. He lets out a long sigh. When he looks back at me, I can tell he's come to a decision. I sit back down at the table, ready to listen.

"When we were younger, my uncle and your father told me to stay away from you. They said life had better things in store for you than a kid like me."

"But that's ridiculous." A spark of anger ignites in me in defense of the boy Andrew was. "There's no one better for me."

He gives a wry smile. "Your father didn't agree. He wanted more." The word *more* is laced with meaning. "More for you. More for himself."

"More?"

Andrew nods. "I stood in the way of that. I always have." He shrugs then pushes the white ceramic mug of coffee to me. "Here. Before it gets cold."

I lift the warm mug and sip. It helps clear the lump from my throat. "But why would he say you're a liar? Or dangerous?"

He takes a long sip from his mug then sets it down on the table. "He never much cared for me."

I furrow my brow. The way he says it makes it sound like a gross understatement.

"I don't like that he was so upset."

Andrew nods and puts his hand on mine. Then he changes

the topic back to the runestone and we start brainstorming on where to begin our search.

Hours later, we're back at Andrew's rental house, sorting through satellite images of the terrain around Romeo's forest. A few years back, archeologists started using high definition satellite images with thermal and infrared capabilities to locate buried settlements, ancient roads, pyramids and burial sites. The satellite images act almost like an X-ray of the earth's surface and let us see places long buried. Entire cities have been uncovered using this technology.

Andrew phoned a contact this morning and had the compiled images sent to him in less than an hour. Not even when Castleton Inc. was at its most prominent did we have that kind of responsiveness. He's really made a place for himself in the field. Just like I knew he would.

We're back in the kitchen, seated at the table. Both of our laptops are open with the satellite images pulled up.

"There's definitely a pre-industrial settlement here." Andrew points to a layered image.

"Yeah. These look like the outlines of longhouses and a turf wall."

Andrew nods, then turns and looks at me. There's a light in his eyes that I recognize. It's the one he used to get when we were hot on the trail of our latest find.

He pulls up a map on the internet and types in the geocoordinates. It pinpoints a location near the forest, close to the field where we were yesterday.

"I'd bet money that Sol's cave is within a mile radius of the settlement."

Andrew nods and uses his mouse to draw a circle. "We'll start our search here then."

A small smile curves on my lips. It's too late in the

afternoon to go today. But we'll be out there first thing in the morning.

"Don't you find it funny..." I look at the map and the outline of the settlement. "The last artifact we found together was made for Queen Isabella, a proclamation of eternal love. And now this artifact is from a husband to his wife. You think the universe is trying to tell us something?"

I raise my eyebrows at Andrew and smile. He was tense for a while after my dad's call. Heck, so was I. But it was forgotten in the excitement of looking through the satellite images.

My phone vibrates in my pocket. I pull it out, expecting an update from Linda, but the caller ID says Justin.

Justin.

I pull in a breath and stand. Andrew looks at me and frowns. "What's up?"

"Sorry. I've got to take this."

I hurry out of the kitchen, walk down the hall and answer his call.

"Hey."

"Em. Your dad called me."

My stomach drops. "Ah. What did he say?"

"That your Andrew is back." Justin's voice is dry.

"Mhmm. Are you okay?" I make it to the end of the hall, it opens into the living room. I stand and look out the window at the landscaped front lawn.

"Well. You know me. I'm pragmatic, logical. I realize that you won't be accepting my proposal."

"No. I can't. I'm sorry." I close my eyes. My heart pinches. I don't love Justin, he knows this. But he's my friend, and I don't want him hurt.

He sighs. "No harm, Em. Look, I'm on my way to Romeo."

"What? You are?" I look out the window as if I expect him to pull up to the drive.

"Your dad was pretty upset. He wasn't making a lot of sense. He asked me to come up, check things over."

"You don't need to do that. Everything is fine. Better than fine."

"Right. I get it. I want you to be happy, Em. But being your friend means I'm going to come up and cross-examine your Andrew, make sure he's good enough for you. Like I said, a person can change a lot in ten years."

I smile ruefully. "You're a wonderful friend. I'm sorry that I couldn't love you. I did try, you know."

He's silent for a moment, then, "I know. I never asked for love, so it's my fault, I suppose. I'll see you in a few hours."

He hangs up and I stand and stare out the window. There's a noise at the entrance to the living room. I turn back and see Andrew leaning against the hallway wall. He's bathed in darkness, and his eyes are dark and unreadable.

"That was Justin Van Cleeve, my friend. You remember him?"

Andrew nods, and once again he reminds me of a cat, ready to pounce on its prey.

I look down at my feet then back at him. I know he isn't sharing everything about his past with me, but I've not been fully forthcoming either.

"He asked me to marry him."

Andrew's eyes grow hooded and he studies me with restrained tension, then, "And what did you tell him?"

"That I can't."

I swallow and wait for Andrew to respond.

He uncoils from the wall and stalks toward me. *Dangerous* flashes through my mind. He looks dangerous. And I remember that's the feeling I got when I first saw him in the woods too.

"What did he say?" he asks in a low voice. He's only a few

feet from me and I can feel the tension coming off of him in heated waves. I step back and my legs hit the back of a low chaise lounge.

"He said he's coming here to see you. He'll be here tonight."

The right side of Andrew's mouth lifts. "He can't have you."

His eyes flick to my mouth, at the freckle above my top lip.

My mouth goes dry.

"No?"

Andrew shakes his head. "No."

"Why not?"

He steps forward, touches his finger to my freckle. He doesn't answer. Instead, he slowly undresses me. Kisses every inch of me until I'm begging him to make love to me. When I can't think, can't form words, he turns me around, unzips his fly, and makes love to me from behind until I'm screaming his name.

Afterword, when I'm dozing off on the chaise in his arms, I realize he never answered my question.

11

ANDREW

EMMA AND I WALK INTO TYBALT'S ITALIAN RESTAURANT AT quarter after seven. I search the interior, dimly lit by candlelight, and find Van Cleeve at a table for four near the back. Emma agreed to meet Justin at seven, but on our way out the door, the sunlight hit the gold in her hair just so, and I had to stop and show her how beautiful I thought she was. That took about half an hour. So, we're a little late.

The restaurant was Emma's suggestion. The interior has a rustic chic authentic Italian vibe. It looks like it could be set down in a historic piazza in a small Italian town and fit right in. In fact, it reminds me of a restaurant I once ate at near Napoli. Emma said her friends recommended it as one of the best places to eat in all of Upstate. By the smells of fresh sauce, yeasty bread and herbs coming from the kitchen I'd guess they're right, but it's hard to concentrate on food when there's another man looking at Emma the way Justin is.

He's smiling at her as if they have a shared history that's years deep.

Then I stiffen because I realize that they do.

They have a history full of shared confidences, mutual support, friendship, perhaps romantic involvement.

I look down at Emma to gauge her reaction. A wide smile spreads over her face and she waves happily at Justin. An ember of jealousy glows in my chest. She looks so carefree and happy. Is that what she's like with him?

Justin stands and raises his hand in greeting.

I take Emma's hand and clasp it in my own. Justin's eyes narrow when I do.

"There's Justin," says Emma. She turns to me. "You okay?"

"Fine," I say. But she raises her eyebrows because it comes out more as a growl. I clear my throat. "Fine."

On the way over she told me more about Justin. He's a prominent lawyer in New York City. He graduated from Columbia Law, lives in a town house near the Natural History Museum, and she visits him multiple times a week. She assured me it was a completely platonic friendship. I wasn't convinced. Now, from the look on Justin's face, I'm even less convinced.

"Welcome to Tybalt's. Do you have a reservation?"

I turn to the hostess, a young woman in a black dress standing behind a tall desk.

"Thank you. We see our party." Emma gestures to Van Cleeve. "We'll see ourselves there."

Emma starts toward Van Cleeve. I take the time to study him. He's clad in a tailored dress shirt, unbuttoned at the collar and rolled up at the sleeves. There's a watch on his wrist that shows off his net worth—high. He has the wavy blond hair, the straight nose, the dimpled good looks, and the open, aww shucks kind of smile that could charm a jury into letting off the devil. I'm not fooled. Van Cleeve's not a man to underestimate.

We get to the table and Emma lets go of my hand. She wraps Justin in a hug. I stand back and try not to look like a mangy dog jealously guarding his bone. When Emma pulls away, Justin turns to me with a cool smile.

He holds out his hand. "Justin Van Cleeve."

I take it and he squeezes harder than necessary. A not so subtle warning. I wasn't completely sure what to expect from him—now I am.

"Andrew Carmichael."

Emma looks at me, then does a double take. I drop Van Cleeve's hand and pull out a chair for Emma. She drops into it and I sit in the seat next to her, across from Van Cleeve. He frowns at our positions at the table. He must've been expecting Emma to sit next to him or across from him. But no. We're at a square table with four chairs, I'm seated across from him, with Emma next to me, diagonal to Van Cleeve.

When we're all seated she turns to me. "When did you change your name?"

Van Cleeve's eyes narrow and he focuses on me like a shark scenting blood.

I shake my head and say in a low voice to Emma. "Never. Santiago was my uncle's last name. Not mine."

Her brows lower and she looks at me for a moment like she wants to pursue the topic and question me more. But then, she seems to remember Justin's presence. She shakes her head and looks back to him.

"Nice to meet you," I say to him.

Justin leans toward me and folds his hands on the table in front of him. "Alright." He shrugs. "You're aware I proposed to Emma?"

Emma makes a choking sound.

I bare my teeth in a facsimile of a smile. He gets straight to the point.

"I'm aware she turned you down."

Justin smiles back, turning on the full force of what I suspect is his courtroom charm. "That's right. She believes you're her soul mate."

"Justin," hisses Emma. I look over at her. Her cheeks are bright red.

Justin ignores her and continues. "Did you pay, bribe, or in any way coerce the woman known as Miss Erma to tell Emma that you are her soul mate?"

I can't help it, I start to laugh.

"Justin. You aren't in court. What's wrong with you?" Emma says.

"Answer the question," he says.

"No. I didn't." I look over at Emma and try to hold back another laugh. Maybe, when all this is through, I'll be able to have a genuine smile again.

It looks like Justin is about to ask another question, but he pauses as our waiter arrives. I order a bottle of wine for the table and antipasto to start. It's always a good idea to have wine and food with verbal sparring.

Emma smiles brightly as the waiter opens and then pours the wine—a Sangiovese. I take a sip and nod my approval. He pours for the table. Emma shifts in her seat. "I can't wait to try the antipasto. I love that they pickle their own vegetables, and I'm such a sucker for Taleggio cheese. Did you know it's been around since Roman times? Even Cicero loved it."

"He did?" I brush my hand over Emma's. I love her history references.

I know this is uncomfortable for her, and she wants Van Cleeve and me to get along. But clearly, there's some things he needs to get out of the way first.

"So. Andrew. Do you or do you not own an island?"

I look at Justin and shake my head. What's with everyone asking about my island? "I do."

"Where?"

"It's a little island off the coast of Belize." I turn to Emma and touch her hand. "I called it Isle Emma. You can only get there by boat. There's a house on the beach. It faces the sunrise. I could take you there."

Emma looks at me and she has that languid expression she gets after making love. "You named it after me?"

I nod. At the time, I named it Isle Emma because I thought it was the only way I'd ever have or want another Emma. But now, it has a different meaning.

Justin interrupts the moment. "And do you or do you not own skyscrapers? And if so where?"

I turn back to Van Cleeve and hold back a scowl. "I do. I own a building in New York City. Two in Singapore. One in London. There are others, but I don't think you actually want to see my portfolio."

"I wouldn't argue if you offered."

He looks over my tailored clothing, the watch on my wrist, and I suspect that the wheels are turning in his head. I'm surprised he hasn't connected me to Dominic yet. Although, maybe he and Dom don't talk business.

"Anyway," says Emma. "Justin, you were right about the Lost Treasure. Andrew and I have found the site where we think it's located."

Justin's left eye twitches, just a fraction, even though his face remains affable. There's his tell.

"Where did you go after the night you disappeared?" he asks, ignoring Emma.

"Mining," I say.

Emma stiffens beside me and I reach out and touch her hand.

"Mining what? Where?"

"Rocks. In the ground. In South America." I give him my cold smile, the one that terrified my fellow prisoners in the mines. It doesn't faze him.

"Why didn't you contact Emma or her father with your whereabouts?"

"I was indisposed."

"For ten years?"

"Yes."

"While you were making"—he rubs his chin and thinks for a moment—"somewhere in the ballpark of half a billion dollars in net worth, you couldn't pick up the phone? Call? Email?"

His ballpark estimate of my worth is low. Not that he needs to know that. Emma looks back and forth between the two of us as we volley words.

"No. I couldn't."

"What is it exactly that you do for a living?" Justin leans back in his chair and crosses his arms over his chest.

The waiter comes and sets the antipasto plate on the table with a flourish. It's full of gourmet cheeses, pickled vegetables, olives, and a selection of homemade breads.

"Have you selected a main course?" the waiter asks.

"I'll have the aged ribeye. She'll have the sea bass," Justin says, nodding at Emma.

Emma glares at Justin. I know for a fact that she loves sea bass. I once caught her one and cooked it over a fire back at camp. But, I also know that she hates it when people tell her what she wants. Justin is trying to make a point, that he knows Emma and is intimate with her likes, but he chose the wrong way to do it.

"Actually. No. I'll have the gnocchi with brown butter, hazelnuts and black truffles." She frowns at Justin and shakes her head.

The waiter turns to me. "Anything for you, sir?"

I start to shake my head no, but Emma kicks my ankle. I didn't look at the menu, so... "I'll have the same. The gnocchi."

When the waiter leaves, Emma leans into me. "Can you spot me for the dinner? I'll pay you back after—"

"You never have to pay me back," I say in a low voice. "For anything."

She flushes.

Justin clears his throat.

"You were telling us about your career? Mining, was it?"

Emma pulls away.

"No. I'm still in the same field as before. I find artifacts."

"But you've branched out into real estate?"

"I have a diverse portfolio."

Justin looks between me and Emma, and I see the moment he realizes that I'm not leaving. That I'm in Emma's life for good.

He switches tactics. "Look, Carmichael. I'm going to be honest. I'm not enthralled that you're back. I have serious concerns about a man who turns up after ten years of being presumed dead, who's now claiming to be as rich as Croesus and my best friend's soul mate. In my field, we'd suspect you of pulling a scam or criminal activity. I don't trust you. And I don't much like you."

"Justin." Emma stands. Both Justin and I stand with her. "Can I talk to you for a moment?"

He nods. Emma walks stiffly to the exit, Justin trails behind her. Through the window I can see Emma talking to him. She's shaking her head and waving her finger. She's reminding me of Boudica again, taking on the Roman army. I pop an olive in my mouth and then take a sip of the wine. Justin holds out his hands and gestures back at me.

The problem is, he's not wrong to be wary of me. I do have a lot to account for. I ruined Castleton, Inc. and even though Emma's dad is the reason I spent five years in hell, Emma didn't deserve the fallout. But how can I tell her that?

Hey, Emma. I spent years planning your destruction. I ruined your business, destroyed your reputation, and caused you to lose your home and all your possessions. You have nothing because of me. Also, your father is a psychopath, my body and soul are covered in scars, and I can't sleep in the dark. Isn't that wonderful? Want to get married?

I shake my head.

Justin has the instincts of a trial lawyer. He's trained to find inconsistencies, to zone in on hesitations and subtle body language and uncover what's hidden.

I gather that he thinks I'm here to hurt Emma. Or scam her. I'm not.

What he's sensing, that hidden thing, is me not knowing how to have a relationship with Emma with all that's behind us. Not knowing how to open up to her.

It's only been a day. But already I see a thousand roadblocks that could prevent us from being together. The big one is that I can't find it in me to be honest with her.

And I don't know how she'll react if she finds out what her father did, and subsequently, what I've done. An objective party would say, just tell her the truth, if she loves you and you're meant to be, it'll all work out.

I scowl down at the table. I'm not much of believer in life working out.

I'd rather her keep believing that her father is a good man, that I wasn't hurt too badly or scarred beyond repair. That she and I can have the life she imagined when we were kids.

I don't ever want to see her hurt.

So, the only route I see forward is keeping her in the dark. I know what Justin would say, what Dominic would say, what I would advise a friend—tell the truth.

But when I think of it, the places Emma lit up inside me start to go dark again.

I can't. Not yet.

The waiter comes and places our meals on the table. I thank him. The truffles fill the air with a savory, nutty, earthy aroma that blends perfectly with the browned butter.

I look out the window. Emma stands with her hands on her hips. Justin shakes his head. It looks like their conversation is coming to a close.

I sit back and watch as they walk back to the table. Emma's cheeks are flushed and Justin's jaw is clenched. I stand and pull out her chair. She sits down, her back ramrod straight.

"This looks delicious," she says.

I sit down next to her.

Justin puts his napkin in his lap and starts sawing at his ribeye with his steak knife.

I pick up my fork and spear a gnocchi. It's soft and tender and melts in my mouth. The truffles are nutty and the brown butter is sweet, Emma was right, it's delicious. Unfortunately, the tension at the table, and my own inability to be forthright, makes it less enjoyable than it should be.

The scraping of Justin's knife against his plate is loud in the silence. He's stiff-backed, but when he looks at me he still has that charming smile on his face.

"Emma mentioned you're renting a house in Romeo."

Did she?

"Yes. A historic home nearby."

"And where do you normally reside?"

Emma looks over at me in curiosity. We hadn't discussed that yet. "I typically stay wherever I'm working."

"For example?"

Emma clears her throat and he raises his eyebrows at her, in an expression that says, *I'm trying to be nice.*

"I was in Singapore recently. I have a place in London. Tangier." I don't mention New York City, I'm not ready to go there yet.

"I always loved Morocco," Emma says. "Do you remember the desert rose you found? I still have it."

The desert rose is a sand crystal that forms in flat petals and looks just like a rose blossom. I gave it to her on our trip through North Africa when I was twelve.

"I remember," I say. A curl of warmth lingers in my chest. There's another reason she loves roses so much. Maybe I can fill her next home with a garden of roses, the flowers and the crystals.

"Will you be staying in the area then? Emma's home is in New York."

I roll my shoulders. "I hadn't made any plans."

"Hmm. Since you mentioned it, what exactly are your plans?" Justin smiles affably.

Emma sets down her fork with a clatter. "It's not your business, Justin."

"I disagree."

Emma goes to stand and I put my hand out to her. She sinks back to her seat. It's obvious she cares about Van Cleeve. It's also obvious she'll cut off their friendship if she thinks he's out of line or believes she has to choose between us. I don't want that.

My instincts tell me he's a good person and he's only trying to protect Emma.

"It's fine," I say. Both Justin and Emma look to me. "Yesterday, I finally found Emma again after ten years of being without. I'm still reeling. Getting my bearings. I don't have a plan."

Justin sets down his utensils and shakes his head. "Funny. You strike me as a man who always has a plan."

I nod. He's perceptive.

"You're right. I plan for Emma and me to find the Lost Treasure. Then I plan for us to be happy. I think we both deserve a bit of happiness."

Emma moves her hand to my thigh and squeezes.

"You may not trust or like me. But I'm grateful to you for being a friend to Emma all these years. Thank you." I hold his gaze. His expression is still mistrustful, but his shoulders relax.

"Alright. Fair enough."

After I pay for dinner we head out to the parking lot.

Emma stops as we walk by a Lamborghini SUV. "Justin's heading back to the city. I'm going to go over to the cabin with him for a quick minute."

Justin leans against the Lamborghini, his hands in his pockets. He watches me carefully.

"I'll come. I can drive you back."

Emma shakes her head. "I need to talk to Justin alone. I won't be long."

Justin opens the passenger side door of his vehicle.

I don't like it, but I trust Emma. She may leave with him but she's coming back to me.

"I'll see you soon."

She slides into the car and lifts her hand. Justin shuts the door.

He starts to walk to the driver's side, then stops in front of me. He eyes me up and down.

Then, "If you hurt Emma, I'll tear you to pieces. You won't even be a footnote in history. If you hurt her, I'll make sure you're destroyed. I don't believe you're the man you claim to be. And when you eff up, I'm going to be there. I'll be the one to help Emma pick up the pieces. Again."

I look at him, acknowledge the truth in his words. "I understand."

The trouble is, I've already hurt Emma. Haven't I?

He leaves, drives Emma back toward the cabin. I stand in the parking lot of Tybalt's, thinking about the inscription on the runestone, the Lost Treasure, and wondering if there really is such a thing as fate and soul mates.

12

Emma

I hold the velvet jewelry box out to Justin. Inside is the heirloom engagement ring he proposed with only a few days ago. "Thank you for being my friend. But I can't accept."

He stands casually, his hands in his pockets. He doesn't reach out to take it. The cabin is cleaner than the last time he was here, and homier. He looks around the small room, then at the bed in the corner with the sheets tucked in and unrumpled.

"Has he asked you to marry him?" he asks. He doesn't look at me when he says it. Instead he walks over to the shelf full of travel knickknacks and runs a finger over a plate from Niagara Falls.

"No. But that doesn't have anything to do with this. We both know I wasn't going to accept. That's independent of Andrew's arrival. I'm sorry, Justin."

He turns and gives me his full-charm grin. "Em, you should try to preserve some of my male pride. Tell me it was a terribly hard decision. You lost many sleepless nights over it. Even now, you struggle with the decision between me, the off-the-charts attractive, good-humored friend and the broody, dark, scarred former flame. Personally, I'd choose the friend." He says this in a way to let me know he's joking

I give a small laugh, but inside I hurt, because I know that our relationship is never going to be the same. We aren't going to be able to have that easy friendship anymore.

"Thank you for understanding," I say.

He shrugs. "I wouldn't be a good friend if I got angry that you rejected my proposal. It wasn't the most romantic thing I've ever done. I just figured friendship was a good basis for marriage. Don't worry about me, Em. I'm fine."

He finally steps close and takes the jewelry box from my hand. He slides it in his pocket. Something shifts in his eyes, behind the humor and the charm. It looks like a hint of sadness, or an acknowledgement of loneliness. Then he shakes it off and the charm is back.

"You can stay here as long as you like." He gestures to the cabin. "Until you know your plans." He says *plans* with a special emphasis. And I remember his line of attack at dinner.

"He's been back a day," I say.

Justin shrugs. "Exactly. As a lawyer I'm going to tell you, he's hiding something. I've seen people on the stand with less guarded behavior."

"I know."

Justin gives me an incredulous look.

"I'm not blind. It just doesn't matter to me. When he's ready he'll tell me what he needs to. He's not a clam that I have to pry open. He'll open up when he's ready."

"Or not."

I nod. "Or not. And that's okay too."

I don't need to make Andrew relive what happened to him

with me. Why would I want to force him to share his trauma? Continually scratching at a wound doesn't make it better. It just causes it to become inflamed. Likewise you can't bury it. No, it's better to just let it go. Whatever way works for him to let it go is okay with me.

Justin sighs and runs his hand through his hair. "Alright. Do you want me to drive you back? Also, please note how much of a good sport I am. Delivering you to the other man. This deserves at least a wine basket at Christmas."

I laugh. But I have to say, "He's not the other man. You and I were never a couple."

"Still. I like the wine baskets with cheese and crackers."

WHEN I GET BACK TO TOWN, ANDREW'S RENTAL HOUSE IS DARK except for a single light in the upstairs bedroom. The front door is unlocked. I close it quietly, lock it and slip off my shoes. The rooms are lit only by moonlight, and a soft glow falls over the antique furniture. I climb up the stairs. They're graceful and sweeping and the varnished wood boards creak under my feet. When I reach the upstairs hall, a small beam of light spills onto the hall floor from the master bedroom.

A warm glow of happiness settles over me and all the worries from earlier fall away. I come to the bedroom and pause at the door.

Andrew is sitting cross-legged on the bed. He's changed into jeans and a long sleeve t-shirt but his feet are bare. I smile because even his feet are tanned, like he's spent long hours barefoot on a beach somewhere. His laptop is in front of him on the bed. He has a line of concentration between his eyebrows and his hair is mussed. The stubble on his face is dark and thicker, and I remember how it felt earlier when he ran it over my breasts.

I must make some noise because Andrew looks up.

When he sees me, his eyes widen in surprise.

Huh. It looks like he didn't think I'd be coming back tonight. Silly man.

"Hey." I casually walk into the bedroom.

He watches me with hungry eyes. "Hey."

I step next to the bed then pull my shirt over my head. His eyes grow dark and fathomless. I drop my shirt then pull my jeans down over my hips. Andrew visibly swallows. His eyes are glued to my breasts.

"You're here." His voice is raspy.

"Mhmm." I climb into the bed next to him. "What're you doing?"

He shakes his head to clear his mind, then tears his eyes from my chest back to his computer. "I was looking at a topographical map of the radius around the settlement, pinpointing likely points for Sol's Cavern."

I look at the screen. There are half a dozen red circles on the map at cavern locations.

Andrew watches me. He's wound as tight as a wire. I keep my eyes on the map. "I gave Justin his engagement ring back. He left for NYC."

I hear Andrew audibly swallow. When I look over at him his eyes are closed and he's letting out a grateful breath. His shoulders visibly relax.

I turn back to the screen before Andrew opens his eyes.

I point to the map. "I think we should start here tomorrow. Work our way out in a concentric circle." I point to the dots as they extend out from the central radius.

"Agreed," he says, his voice raw. Then he carefully takes his laptop, closes it and sets it on the nightstand.

When he turns to me, his eyes are full of hungry fire. The way he touches me, gentle and slow, is at odds with the heat in his eyes. He pulls free my panties and bra and kisses me until I'm burning as hot as he is. When I open his pants and set him free, he pushes me down and enters me in one fast stroke.

"Emma. My Emma." He takes my mouth and thrusts his tongue in time to him entering me. I want to tell him that I'll never leave him, that I'll stay with him forever, that he doesn't have to worry or be afraid of what I'll think or say, that whatever happened in the past is okay. I want to tell him all of this, but I'm caught up in the feel of him inside me, his mouth over mine, and all the words are lost. So instead, I show him and I use the only words I have left.

"I love you," I say. "I love you."

He thrusts harder and faster, tilts up my hips until I'm coming around him.

Then, when I'm finished, he pulls my naked body close. Wraps his arms around me. The warmth of his still-clothed body and the blankets covering me lull me to sleep in the bright light of the room.

13

———

Andrew

It's growing close to dusk. In less than an hour the sun will set. Emma and I are hiking in the woods, nearly a mile from the buried settlement. We spent the entire day searching the caverns that I mapped out last night and have only two more to go. We didn't go far inside any of the caves. None of the previous four seemed likely as Sol's Cavern. They were either too shallow, stopping in a wall of rock near the entrance, or too narrow. I'm expecting to find a landform similar to what Vikings left in other locations. Large, wide, circular caverns that let in light through narrow shafts.

Ahead of me, Emma wipes a drop of sweat from the back of her neck. She's in jean shorts, a t-shirt, a baseball hat, and hiking boots.

We brought day packs with utility tools and flashlights, food, plenty of water, and bug spray. I'm most grateful for the bug spray. It rained last night and the mosquitos are thirsty.

The woods are gathering into the noisy, busy period before dark. The forest birds sing and fly about, a deer runs by, and the horseflies are biting. I smack at one on my arm.

"Want to call it a day?" Searching the caves during the daylight was fine, it didn't bring up many memories. But the idea of going into one with dark falling is causing tension to ride up into my shoulders and back.

Emma looks back and smiles. "We're only a hundred meters from the next. Let's just check it and see. Then we can hike out and I'll make dinner." At the word *dinner* she presses her lips together and flushes.

I stare at her mouth and decide that braving a cave at dusk is well worth dinner and anything else she has in mind. We've spent the day exploring the woods and each other. She's asked questions about my business and I've told her a little more about what I do.

How I now specialize in finding items of value in everyday places, the lost items in plain sight. I told her about my auction house and my partnership with Dom. She asked a lot of questions, brought up points I hadn't thought of and offered ideas for where we might streamline and where we could expand. I imagined it was the case before, but now I know, Emma has a keen business mind and a real instinct for how to move in the marketplace. I think if I hadn't sabotaged her progress, she would've made Castleton, Inc. even more successful than her father did.

She'll start again though. I don't think there's much of anything in the world that can hold her down. She started to articulate that she might like to stay here and excavate the settlement – it'll take years to carefully remove the layers of soil and uncover the history buried in the site. She's always loved the process of discovery best. But then, during her story, she looked over at me and something made her stop. Then she shrugged and said the future was up in the air.

I'd be lying if I said that didn't unsettle me.

This morning, when she put my laptop into my briefcase, the file folder with the printed report slipped out. Her hand paused over her name printed on the folder's edge.

"What's this?" she asked with a smile. "Were you doing research on me too?"

"Yes," I said. Then I kissed her and pushed the file back into my bag.

Emma seems to have forgotten it, but I haven't. I can't keep this up much longer. Last night in bed, I wanted so badly to uncover myself to her, let her see me as I am. But I couldn't. Didn't.

Up ahead, I can see the shadowed outline of a large rocky outcropping. It's covered in moss and vines. The sun is nearing the horizon and the golden light hits the stone and turns it a burnished gold.

"My word," Emma breathes. She stops and stares at the light glistening over the cave. "Do you think...?"

She turns to me with a question in her eyes.

Sometimes, ancient people would have the entrance shafts of caverns or burial mounds face the sunset or sunrise so that when the sun hit it just right, the interior room of the cave would be bathed in a golden glow. It's a magical experience. They believed that the deads' souls could fly up on the beam of light and be set free.

This cave's entrance faces due west, toward the setting sun.

"There's only one way to find out," I say.

We hurry forward into the woods, trying to beat the sun before it sinks below the horizon. I push aside the plant growth near a two-foot-tall entrance and find a rune carved into the stone.

"It says Sol." I look over at Emma.

She touches the rune. There's a look of awe on her face. Then she turns to me and there's joy in her eyes. "We found it."

Suddenly, I'm taken back to another place. The cenote, *The Heart*, Emma saying the same words. At that time, I knew she loved me, and I'd felt like I could fly. Like I was free. I want to feel that again.

I grin at her, all the past falling away. I can feel that again.

Emma blinks, looks at me with a stunned expression.

"I haven't seen you smile like that since..."

I can't pull the smile back. It's all going to be alright. "I know. Come on."

I duck down and crawl into the low cavern. Emma crawls in behind me. The tunnel is circular and smooth, like it was carved out with iron tools. After only four feet of crawling I reach the end of the tunnel and step into the cavern. Emma stands up behind me.

The room is about twenty feet in circumference and fifteen feet high. The walls are limestone and the ground is rock and dirt. Emma stands next to me and presses into my side.

"Do you see what I'm seeing?" she asks.

We turn in a slow circle, taking it all in. Suddenly, the light from the setting sun hits the entrance tunnel and the cavern is filled with a golden glow.

"The Lost Treasure," I say.

"It's beautiful." She wraps her arms around me and we both take in the shining gold room. I think the ancient people were right. At this moment, I do feel as if my spirit can fly free.

"What does it say?" Emma whispers.

I look at the elegantly carved runes and the intricate scrollwork meticulously inscribed into the cavern walls. The runes circle the cave and are illuminated in the light. I begin to read.

"It's a love poem." I say. I lean down and kiss Emma on the top of her head. "My love, kiss me. Kiss me."

I brush a kiss across her forehead, she tilts her head up, her skin is washed in gold. Her lips are partly open to me, so I reach down and drag my mouth over hers. I don't have to look up to know the next line.

I whisper it against her lips. "Remember me always, I remember you."

She wraps her arms around my shoulders and leans into me. This is Romeo's Treasure. Not gold, or Viking spoils, jewels, or crowns—it's the love of a man for his wife.

She brushes her fingers over my face, runs her hands down my cheeks, my throat, to my beating heart.

"Is there more?"

I nod and press my hand over hers. I look at the inscription and then back into her eyes.

"Love me," I say. "I love you."

Her lips tremble and her hand presses into my chest. Even though I'm reading the words from an inscription on the wall, I'm speaking them from my heart.

"I love you so much that even fire seems cold. Kiss me, my love. Remember me. I remember you."

My throat is raw, and I realize that there are tears in my eyes. I can't look away from her. We stand in the center of Romeo's Lost Treasure, an ancient work of art bathed in golden sunlight, and I can't look away from Emma.

"I love you too," she whispers.

A great feeling of relief washes through me and I feel as if a thousand pounds has been lifted from me.

"I love you. I love you."

I drop my forehead to hers and close my eyes. Our breath mingles and I press my lips to hers.

"Marry me. Marry me, Emma."

"Is that part of the poem?"

I look down at her and smile. "No. That's me asking you to be my wife. To stay with me forever. To kiss me. To love me. To be mine."

"Yes," she says. "Always, my answer is always yes."

I take her mouth in mine, and as we kiss I taste tears. And I don't know whether they're hers or mine. Then I pull her shirt from her head, lift it off and drop it to the ground. She looks up at me, a question in her eyes, and I nod. She takes my long-sleeve t-shirt and pulls it off me. The golden light illuminates the white raised lines covering my skin. They crisscross over me, as thick as a wicked spiderweb.

I look to Emma's eyes and swallow down the fear I have at her reaction.

She nods her head once, slowly. "Okay," she says. A single tear falls down her cheek, but she doesn't wipe it away. She keeps her eyes on mine. Then she presses her hands to my chest and places a kiss over my heart. "You came back to me," she whispers. "I'm so glad you came back to me."

She kneels down in front of me and slowly unties my shoes. She pulls them off. Then she unbuttons my jeans and pulls them down my legs. They are even more scarred then my chest and back. If my legs were hurt, I'd be less likely to run.

I watch her face. Even with her head bent I can still see her expression.

There's no pity, no revulsion. Only acceptance. And love. My word. There's so much love there.

"Emma." My voice breaks on her name. I try to say everything in that one word.

She nods and puts her lips over my length. I throw back my head from the pleasure and the pain of it. She pulls on me and I reach for her. Pull her to me.

I can't...

I need...

I yank her clothes from her. Make a pile on the ground and love her. With each thrust I tell her. "I love you."

I feel free.

When we're both sated, laying in a pile on our clothing, I realize that all the light is gone. The cavern is dark.

But I don't feel any fear. In fact, laying in the dark, with Emma in my arms, I only feel love.

14

Emma

He loves me. *He wants to marry me.*

I rest my head on Andrew's chest and wrap my arms around him. The air is cooler here than in the forest, but Andrew is warm, so I curl into him. He lays on his back on the pile of our clothing, completely relaxed. I press my face into his neck and breathe in the heat of him. I love him so much.

I rub my hands over his shoulders, his chest and arms. I can feel the thin scars as I pass my hands over him. I stroke him gently, sweep the sadness of them away, like an archeologist with their brush, meticulously removing the dusty layers.

He came back to me. Seeing what he suffered, it's a miracle that he's here.

What he doesn't realize is that I would take him any way he came to me, scarred or not, rich or poor...in good times and bad, for better or for worse.

The cavern light has faded. Andrew runs his hand over the

curve of my hip and then rests it at the base of my spine. A warm pulse deep inside me responds to his touch. I feel tethered to him.

"This is the first time I've been in the dark since escaping the mine."

I shift and look up at him, but his face is completely shadowed. "You haven't..."

He pulls me closer. "No. Every time I tried I'd feel like I was suffocating, like I was being buried alive. I couldn't breathe, I'd break out in a sweat. I'd go senseless with fear until I turned the light back on. I never lasted more than fifteen seconds. I haven't been in the dark in almost five years."

I reach up and brush my hand over his face and through his hair. "What happened?"

"I found something that scared me more than the fear."

"What?"

"Losing you."

I move up and brush my mouth across his lips. "You won't lose me. I'm right here."

He leans into me, buries his face in my hair and takes a deep shuddering breath.

"How's this," I say. "If either of us ever gets lost, all we have to do is come back here. That's what this place is for isn't it? Finding your true love again?"

He makes a noise of assent and presses his mouth against mine. Finally he pulls away.

"I didn't think I'd ever be with you again," he says. His voice is low and rough, like the edges of the sandstone surrounding us.

"Me either."

"When we were young, everyone said you shouldn't be with me because I was a former street kid and destined to go nowhere. Now, people will say you shouldn't be with me because I'm broken."

I make a noise of disagreement.

"It's the truth, Emma. I'm broken. I spent five years crawling like an animal through a mine, chained to five other miserable souls, prying loose emeralds. If you couldn't walk into the mine, you died. If you didn't bring out your quota, you died. My uncle was murdered in the first year, by Crudell. I called him and his lackeys the wardens. There were a dozen prisoners, sometimes two dozen, always there. Always chained."

I curl into him and hold him. I want to reassure myself that he's here, with me.

"Storms would come and the rain would wash down the mountain and fill the mine. Once all five of the men chained to me drowned. I don't know how or why I lived. It took me fifteen hours to drag their bodies out. I felt then that it was a blessing that my uncle died so early on. He never had to see the horrors of it."

Andrew continues, his voice a quiet whisper, like he's afraid to say what happened out loud. I press my hand against his cheek.

"I tried to escape. Eighteen times. I wanted desperately to get back to you. Each time, Crudell held me for days. He was creative in the ways he tried to dissuade me from running."

"No. Andrew." I press my forehead to his. "I'm so sorry. I should've looked harder. I should've tried harder. I...I failed you."

"You haven't." He sits up and pulls me into his lap. Wraps his arms around me. "Just by being you, staying you, you've done more than I could've ever hoped."

I lean into him and soak up his warmth. Then I say, "You may have conquered the dark. But I was hoping you wouldn't mind if I spent every night starting now with you."

I feel him smile against my cheek. "I don't mind. In fact, I demand it."

"We should get married."

He lets out a laugh, "I already asked. You said yes."

"I mean this week, or next. I don't want to wait."

He presses a kiss to my mouth. "I was hoping you'd say that."

I WAKE UP SPOONED IN ANDREW'S ARMS IN HIS KING BED BACK AT the rental house. There's a loud banging on the door. I growl then moan, "Go away." My eyes are gritty and I realize I'm not going to wake up without a healthy dose of coffee.

The knocking continues. I look over my shoulder at Andrew. He's still asleep. Looks like persistent knocking isn't something that'll wake him. I slip out from under his arm and scoot to the edge of the bed. The sunrise is just starting to filter through the curtains. So, it's six-ish. In the morning.

The knocking stops and I let out a sigh of relief. But then, my cell phone starts vibrating. It's in my shorts pocket on the floor. Suddenly, my chest tightens. This isn't some random jerk pounding on the door at the crack of dawn. Someone's trying to reach me. I hop off the bed and yank my cell phone out my shorts pocket. It's Justin.

"Hello?"

"Emma. I'm at the door. Open up, for crying out loud."

I look back at Andrew. Still asleep. His arm is thrown over the spot where I was lying and his head is resting on my pillow. I throw on my shorts and my tank top.

"What is it?" I move back toward the bed to wake up Andrew.

"Linda and I have been calling for hours. What have you been doing? Em, it's your dad."

At his words, I forget about waking Andrew. I rush from the room and run down the stairs. When I yank open the front door I find Justin standing there. I drop my phone. His eyes are bloodshot and he has bags under them. He's in a wrinkled t-shirt and jeans, and his hair is a mess. I've never seen him like this. Not even after the benders he did studying for the bar or the sleepless weeks before his first big trial.

A pulse of panic rolls over me.

"What happened. Is he—"

I can't say it. He can't be dead.

"No. No. Can I come in? I left the city just after two to get here. I've been driving all night."

A small wash of relief moves through me. My dad's not dead. But it is something serious. Otherwise Justin wouldn't have left in the middle of the night to reach me.

"Right. Come in. I'll get coffee. You can sit down."

I lead him to the kitchen and flip on the automatic coffeemaker.

"What happened, Justin? Please, I'm really freaked out."

He nods. "Linda called me last night. Your dad had another stroke. He's not doing well. He needs you there. He made me promise to bring you back."

"Of course I'll come." I press my hand to my stomach. Dad's been getting weaker and I knew that his time was going to come soon. "Of course I'll come. I just have to grab some clothes from the cabin."

Justin looks at my face and his softens in sympathy. "Hey. It'll be alright."

I nod and hold back my tears. He's right. This has happened before. It'll be okay this time too.

"Come here," he says. He holds open his arms.

I walk into them and hug him back. "Thank you for coming."

"Of course I came."

"Hello, Van Cleeve. I didn't know we were expecting company," Andrew says.

I look toward the hall. Andrew leans in the kitchen doorway, deceptively casual. He raises an eyebrow at Justin. I see the same light in Andrew's eyes that he had after he made love to me in the living room. He's not happy to see Justin here. Not at all.

Justin slowly pulls back from me and nods at Andrew. "Morning," he says in a neutral voice.

Andrew is fully dressed in jeans and a long-sleeve shirt. When I left him he was naked and still sleeping. He must've woken up, realized I was gone, thrown on his clothes and rushed down the stairs.

My heart pinches at the thought that he might've been worried that I left him. I walk over to him, take his hand and pull him into the kitchen. He eyes Justin with wariness and suspicion. Justin remains stoically distant.

"Andrew," I say. I squeeze his hand. "Justin drove all night to get here. My dad—" My voice falters and I choke on the last word.

Andrew turns quickly and focuses his entire attention on me. "What happened?" He takes both my hands. "Are you okay?"

I press my lips into a firm line and nod my head yes.

The coffeemaker beeps. The pot is full of morning roast. Justin walks over and pulls down three mugs from the glass-fronted cabinet. He pours three cups of coffee and then sets them down on the counter in front of us.

Andrew looks at Justin and the coffee and then nods his

thanks. He pushes a mug toward me. "Drink," he says. Then he turns to Justin. "What happened?"

I look down and wrap my hands around the steaming mug.

Justin speaks in a perfunctory tone. "Last night at nine p.m. Mr. Castleton's full-time nurse phoned me after she failed in her attempts to reach Emma. She made me aware that Mr. Castleton was seeking emergency medical care for a stroke. I don't have any updates on his condition. The last I heard was at midnight when Linda informed me it would be prudent if Emma came as quickly as possible. I left shortly after."

I feel Andrew stiffen beside me. He reaches out and puts a hand to my lower back. I close my eyes and drop my chin. It trembles and I clamp my teeth together.

"I'll take you," Andrew says. "We can go together."

"No," Justin says.

I feel Andrew's hand tense on my back. I open my eyes. Andrew and Justin are locked in a battle of wills. They aren't moving, but their eyes say a whole lot more than words could express.

Justin breaks eye contact first. He looks at me.

"Linda told me that learning of Andrew's return sent your father into a decline. She feels it would be extremely detrimental for your father's health to see Andrew. Or even for you to mention him. Linda thinks his presence could tip the scales—"

"That's ridiculous," I cry. Stupid, idiotic, ridiculous.

Andrew puts a staying hand on my arm. "No. He's right. If my presence upsets your father then I shouldn't be there."

I frown and look up at him. "But it doesn't make any sense."

He smiles at me ruefully. "It doesn't have to make sense. Your father is important to you, his health is important, therefore, it's important to me. Go." He nods to the door. "You'll be back by tomorrow or the next day. Your dad will be fine."

I shake my head but he takes my hands and squeezes them. "You'll be back tomorrow or the next day," he repeats more firmly, "and then we'll do that thing we discussed."

His eyes are deep and full of yearning. He means we'll get married. I'll come back and we'll get married. My shoulders relax and I nod.

"Okay," I say.

He smiles and I'm filled with happiness when I realize it's a real smile that touches his eyes.

"Good," he says. "It's a deal."

"Will you stay here while I'm gone?" I'd like to think I'm coming back to him and our Lost Treasure in Romeo.

"I think I'll be able to keep myself busy," he says. He lets my hands go and nods his head toward the door. "You better head out."

Before I turn to go, I reach over and give him a kiss goodbye.

15

———

After a four-hour drive filled with tension and uncertainty, Justin and I make it to my dad. Linda called when we were two hours north of NYC to let us know he was at home.

Home is an assisted living community on the banks of the Hudson River. Dad moved in two years ago after he became too weak to manage day-to-day activities on his own. There are apartments, town homes and ranch houses in the development, as well as doctors and nurses on staff at a clinic in the main building.

Dad has his own ranch-style house with an apartment off the back for Linda. We used the money in my mom's trust to purchase it and pay for his care—thank goodness, because otherwise he would have lost this in the bankruptcy. I don't know what I would've done if that had happened. He's never liked it here, he hates the golf course, the pool, the inability to work—he hates it all. But I think he'd hate it worse if he was forced to leave.

When Justin pulls into the drive I jump out of the car and run in the front door without knocking. Linda is sitting in the front room, on the sofa, reading a magazine. When I rush in she looks up at me and blinks owlishly at the bright afternoon light coming in. All the curtains are drawn and the house is dark and quiet.

"Is he alright? Where is he?" I ask.

Linda dog-ears the page of the magazine and then sets it aside.

She's middle-aged with a few gray streaks in her hair. She's always in floral scrubs and white shoes, and she has the uncanny ability to never be ruffled by anything. Right now, I'd like to shake her. She's kept us in suspense for hours, meanwhile she's been reading on the couch and...I glance at the coffee table...sipping a cup of tea.

Linda stands and smooths out her scrubs. "I'll take you. He's in his office."

Justin walks in just as I start to follow Linda. He shuts the door behind him. I motion for him to follow. As we walk through the hushed house, I wonder why my dad is in his office if he just had a serious stroke. And why isn't Linda with him?

Linda leads us through the hallway. The house is bare of any personal touches. Dad never wanted to decorate it. He said there was no point in decorating a home that was his last stop. He used to have maps, African masks, spears, coins and more hanging on the walls of his other homes. Not here. He didn't want a reminder of what his life used to be. Plus, it was all auctioned off to pay our debts.

The walls are beige and the carpet is a slightly darker beige. On my left is the kitchen. The countertops are sand-colored quartz and the cabinets are a lighter sand color. On the right is the first of two bedrooms with an en-suite handicap-accessible bath and more sandy beige used in decorating than I saw in the Sahara Desert.

Linda stops in front of the office door and knocks lightly.

"Come." It's my dad's voice. Linda opens the door for us but doesn't go in.

I step into the room and Justin follows. Behind us Linda quietly shuts the door.

I pause and look at my dad. He's sitting upright at his broad, dark wood desk in his leather desk chair. He's slumped slightly to the left and he looks tired, but I don't see any evidence that he's worse off physically than he was when I saw him two weeks ago.

The only difference that I can see is that instead of his usual hard, cool-eyed expression, he looks like a pit bull about to tear into an intruder. His face is an uncomfortable shade of purple, his mouth is tight and his eyes are bloodshot and angry.

"Dad? What is it?"

"Emma. Good. You got out of the viper's den." He scowls, and I watch as he sets shaking

hands down in front of him on the desk.

What in the world?

I turn to look at Justin. Does he know anything about what's going on? But he shakes his head and raises his eyebrows. He's just as confused as I am.

"Mr. Castleton, you look well. I'll just be out—"

"Sit down, Emma," my dad interrupts. "Justin, glad you're here. You can stay."

"What in the world is going on, Dad? Linda said you had another stroke. I was scared—"

My dad holds up his hand and I stop.

"I'll explain. Sit down, please."

I look back to Justin. He shrugs. I move to one of the chairs in front of my dad's desk and perch on the end of the cushion. Justin comes and leans against the back of the other. I'm glad he's here. He has that alert, lawyer-like stance, which means his mind is working fast to figure out what the heck is going on.

Because one thing is incredibly clear. My dad didn't have a stroke last night. Linda lied. My dad lied.

I take a breath and try to fill my tight chest. The curtains in the room are drawn and the heavy atmosphere is making me nervous. "Okay. Explain. And then apologize. Justin drove all night to get me. He missed a day in court, I'm missing a day at my site—"

My dad's face splotches a darker shade of purple and red. "I had to get you away from him. You wouldn't go if I told the truth. He's dangerous."

My stomach drops, and suddenly I realize what this is about. My dad's irrational distrust of Andrew. I close my eyes and let go of all the worry I had for my dad. But anger replaces it. I lean forward in my chair and pin my dad with a hard stare.

"You tricked Justin and me because you wanted to get me away from Andrew? For crying out loud. That's not acceptable, Dad. That's not okay."

Next to me, Justin straightens and steps back from the chair. He's no fool, he knows when to exit a family disagreement.

"Dad, I love you, but there's something you need to accept. I love Andrew. He loves me."

My dad flinches as if I struck him.

I make my voice softer. Apparently my dad doesn't want to hear this, but he needs to. "Andrew asked me to marry him. I said yes."

My dad's face drains of color. "He's sicker than I thought. He'll stop at nothing."

My mouth drops open. Justin clears his throat uncomfortably. "I'll just wait in the car."

"Stay," my dad says in a harsh whip-like voice. "I'm hiring you as legal counsel."

"Legal counsel?" I look between my dad and Justin. Justin's eyes narrow on my dad.

My dad's hands shake as he pulls open his top desk drawer and removes a thick file. "I had to get you out of there without Santiago, or Carmichael as he calls himself, knowing that you were aware of his actions." My dad drops the file on his desk and it hits the surface with a hard thud. My stomach clenches. I look at the file like I would a pit of snakes. I don't want anywhere near it.

"Andrew hasn't done anything to me. He's not dangerous. He's not out to hurt me. I don't know what you have against him, but it doesn't matter to me." I scoot back in my chair. "Nothing you have to say will change my feelings."

I know Andrew went through hell, I know it scarred him, and I know he believed that I was responsible. But all of that is in the past.

My dad's eyes are red-rimmed and bloodshot. The anger in them has softened and he looks at me with an expression tinged with pity. It's the same pitying look he gave me when he told me my mom was gone. Then he was younger, stronger— my indefatigable dad. Now he's stooped, slumped and weakened. White-haired and made bitter by the twists of life. But the look he's giving me is the same.

I press a hand to my stomach.

He opens the folder. Justin moves closer and rests his hand on the back of my chair. An offer of silent support.

"Andrew Santiago, now known as Andrew Carmichael, is the business partner of Dominic Sato. They own Suffolk Auction House."

Behind me, Justin stiffens. "I'll be..." he says. "How'd I miss that?"

My dad's eyes flick up to Justin. "Because he wanted you to."

I shrug. "I already know this. Andrew told me. He's successful. You should be proud."

My dad takes a stack of photographs from the top of the folder. They look like grainy screenshots from a low-tech security camera. A younger, much thinner and more haggard Andrew is sitting on a barstool. Even in an image of such poor quality, I can tell that Andrew is sick, nearly starved. He perches on a stool next to a lean, brown-haired man in a linen suit. "The two met in a bar in Cartagena. *Santiago* had one hundred thousand dollars' worth of uncut emeralds on him, likely stolen, and a vendetta."

I stare at the image of Andrew and I have the strongest urge to run back to him and hold him. It physically hurts to see him like that, with shoulders stooped and head bowed. I feel sick that my dad felt he had to pry into Andrew's past and expose him like this. "I know all this, Dad. Andrew told me. He thought I betrayed him. He wanted revenge."

My dad stops and looks at me sharply. "He didn't want it," he says in a choked voice. "He got it."

"What?" I shake my head.

My dad starts to shake and cough, then I realize that he's laughing. I look up at Justin. He lowers his brows. He seems worried. My dad's laugh slows and he carefully spreads pages and pages of documents out in front of him.

"After Santiago left Colombia he styled himself a new man. Carmichael. He spent five years building wealth, contacts, prestige. He was relentless in hunting us, laying traps, and systematically destroying us. I wondered how a business I spent thirty-five years building could collapse so quickly. Until I realized it didn't fall. It was pushed. Your Andrew destroyed us. Destroyed you."

I shake my head. I'm having trouble believing what my dad is saying. "That's ridiculous."

My dad pushes a page in front of me. "Morocco. Five years ago." It's Andrew shaking hands with an official I recognize and a memo from the official stating that doing business with Castleton, Inc is against their interests. Our permit for that dig was rejected. My dad pulls out more documents and rattles off a long list of countries, dig sites, museums and private collectors that we'd been blackballed from in the past five years. I'd thought it was random bad luck. Or that people didn't like working with me as much as my dad. I thought it had been my fault that our client base dried up. It wasn't.

With each new page he sets down, I'm less able to deny what I'm seeing.

Andrew spent years, *years*, working to destroy me.

But...

The papers on the desk start to blur and I blink them back into focus.

He didn't know. He was hurting. He...

I look at the stack of papers still waiting in the file and I start to feel ill. There's more. "What else?" I ask, and my tongue feels thick and heavy.

"He orchestrated a set of rumors and misinformation to encourage you to make bad investments and take on hefty debts for ventures that turned out to be hoaxes." My dad sets down a series of papers. They flutter before me. I don't pick them up. "Denmark. Wyoming. Chad. Guatemala."

I stare at the page he holds up. It's the site of my last dig. Where I authenticated the find. Where it was then discovered that I'd given the museum a forgery. "I have it on good authority that he placed the forgery at the site. He set you up."

The word *"fake"* flashes in my mind. My picture was

plastered on newspapers around the world with fake stamped on my face, painting me as a desperate, crooked swindler.

I feel my face drain of color. Andrew did that? He spent five years tearing me down?

"I'll kill him," growls Justin. "I will take the bastard apart."

"But..." I say. My body is cold and my mind feels like a blanket has been thrown over it. Nothing makes sense and I can't form a coherent thought. "He didn't. He wouldn't."

I think of him just last night, the love and yearning in his face. But then I think of the file with my name on it in his briefcase. I'd laughed it off, but he admitted to having researched me. He also admitted to wanting revenge. To staying away for five years even though he could've contacted me at any time.

I look back up at my father. His face is grim. "The financials." He holds up a sheaf of documents. "Proof of his influence on our financial collapse. This is his shell company. He bought up our debts and then called them in. The foreclosures were his doing."

The image of my mother's rose garden flashes in my mind. Andrew took it away?

My dad holds up another stack of documents. "Proof of his campaign to cut off our permits, museum contacts and goodwill with private collectors."

I slump forward on the seat and wrap my arms around my stomach.

My dad waves another pile.

"I don't want to hear it," I say. I don't want to hear any more.

Why did he do this?

And why didn't he tell me?

The foreclosures and my last dig, where I was labeled a fraud, they all happened less than a month ago. Weeks even.

He couldn't have worked for five years toward my

destruction, seen the culmination and then just turned around and changed his mind about me. He saw me ruined and then two days later found me in the woods? And declared his love?

My dad slides another sheet of paper across the desk and sets it in front of me.

"His permit request for the dig in Romeo, submitted shortly after your own. He didn't arrive by coincidence, Emma," my dad says in a hard voice. "A week ago he witnessed the destruction of your career, your life. He came to finish what he started."

I look up at my dad and his eyes turn soft with pity. "Emma. He doesn't want to marry you, he wants to break you. A man like that doesn't love. He destroys."

I close my eyes and drop my head. My hands clench in my lap so hard that my knuckles begin to ache.

He destroyed me. He ruined me. He…

I open my eyes and look at the picture of Andrew in the bar in Cartagena. I can see the dark shadowy blur of his eyes. He looks so broken. Barely alive. I reach out and brush my fingers over his face.

Oh Andrew.

How much they hurt you.

"We'll bring him down," Justin says. "He won't get away with this."

I rest my hand over the photograph then look up at my dad. "I don't agree with you. He has plenty of love to give."

My dad's brows lower and his face turns splotchy. "Emma. The bastard spent five years working to destroy you. Now he's trying to break you through some sick scheme. Ruining your career and finances wasn't enough."

Justin clears his throat. "I hate to say it, Em, but Edward's right. I don't think his intentions toward you are honorable."

I pull my phone from my pocket. "The last I heard, in this

country we go by the tenet innocent until proven guilty. I'm not interested in a one-sided pitchfork mob."

I hit Andrew's number and put the phone to my ear. I stand up and walk to the other side of the office. I face away from Justin and my dad and look at the empty bookshelves. I let the phone ring a dozen times, twenty. It never goes to voice mail, it just keeps ringing. My heart thunders in my chest. I need him to answer. I hang up then dial again. The phone rings on and on.

Finally, I tap disconnect and slide the phone in my pocket. I take a breath and turn back to my dad.

He looks at the tear running down my cheek and scowls.

Justin walks to me and puts his hand to my arm. "I'm sorry."

I shake my head and shrug his hand off my arm. He gives me a look of surprised hurt.

He frowns, then snaps his fingers and gives me a reassuring smile. "Here. I'll settle this. I'll call Dom. We'll figure this out."

Justin pulls out his phone and flips through his contacts. Then he dials and puts it on speakerphone. Dom picks up on the third ring.

"Justin. What's up? You calling about Friday? We still on for tennis?"

Justin watches me as he talks. "Dominic. I'm here with Emma and Edward Castleton. We're on speaker. I wanted to ask you a few questions about your partner, Andrew Carmichael."

There's a short silence on the other end, then Dominic says, "Ah. I see." His voice has leached of the warmth that was there earlier.

Justin raises his eyebrows. "I was wondering if you're aware of any interest your partner may have or have had in Miss Emma Castleton or her father, Edward."

Dominic clears his throat. I hold my breath and wait for his response. From the way Andrew spoke so fondly of Dom, I think that he'll tell Justin that Andrew cares for me and Justin should quit being a lawyerly prick. Dom will set him and my dad straight.

"Well?" asks Justin.

"I think," says Dom, "that you should address any questions to our in-house legal team. Shall I forward you to them?"

Justin's mouth flattens into a thin line. My dad watches him with hawk eyes.

"No. That won't be necessary," says Justin.

"Fair enough."

"I'll see you Friday for tennis?" asks Justin in a cagey tone. I frown at him. Why is he asking about tennis after a call like this?

"No. I don't think that's a good idea," says Dom. His voice has lost all warmth.

I start to feel short of breath. This isn't right. This isn't normal.

"Take care then," says Justin.

They disconnect.

My dad leans back in his chair. His shoulders are slumped. He should look tired, but instead he looks vindicated.

Justin stares at the screen on his phone and shakes his head.

"What exactly did that conversation mean?" I ask.

Justin looks up at me and I can tell that he feels sorry for what he's about to say. "It means, Em, that Carmichael is as guilty as sin."

My chest cracks and I feel like my heart and all the happiness from this morning spills out. "What? Why?"

"Dom's circling the wagons. Calling in the lawyers. He knew about Carmichael and whatever he intends. He just gave me fair warning."

My dad gives a wheezing laugh. "I've already notified my

contacts in the media. They're running the story today. We'll destroy him in court."

What? No. I shake my head. "No."

Both Justin and my dad look at me.

"No," I say again. "That's not what I want."

"Emma," my dad begins to argue.

"No."

I look down at the picture of Andrew. Maybe he started out with revenge as a goal, but he didn't end there. If he can forgive and move on from what happened in the mine, I can move on from this.

A sudden niggling makes me look at my dad. Then I ask a question that surprises me, even as I ask it. "Did you hire Crudell to take Andrew? Are you the reason he was in the mines?"

My voice is high and I feel short of breath. When I see my dad's resolute expression I know the answer.

"You did," I say.

I lean down and grasp the edge of his desk. I think of Rigo's death, of Andrew's scars, his fear and the terror he lived through and I have trouble staying upright.

"You did this to him." I look at my dad and I feel sick. "Why?" I cry.

My dad clenches his trembling hands into fists and squares his shoulders. His breathing becomes more rapid and his nostrils flare. He's not going to answer.

"Dad. Why?"

He lets out a choking breath. "You were going to quit school. Live in a hut. You would've given up your place in life to live in squalor with a street rat."

I stare at him as the full import of what he'd done hits me. "Rigo died. Andrew was imprisoned for years. I was..." I choke off. I can't continue.

"I didn't tell Crudell how to treat him. That's not my doing. I only told Crudell to keep him busy and away from us. I did it for you. To protect you."

Holy...

I shake my head. "No. You did it to protect yourself."

His face blanches. "He's a monster. He's proven himself a monster. I was right."

"Goodbye, Dad."

I look at Justin. "I'm going. Will you drive me back to Romeo?"

He looks at me, weighs what I'm saying, and then gives a nod. "Right. Okay."

I turn my back on my dad and head to the door. Back toward Andrew.

"Emma. Don't turn your back on me. Don't...don't..." He starts to wheeze again, then, "Emma. Don't." His words start to slur. I stop. Justin stops next to me.

"Emma," my dad slurs.

Then I hear him slump in his chair.

I turn around.

The left side of his face has gone slack. He tries to choke out a word, can't, and then he falls forward onto his desk.

16

———————

Andrew

This is undoubtedly the happiest day of my life.

Emma has agreed to be my wife. I love her and she loves me. I shared with her my past, my scars, and my fears, and she accepted me. Even my worry over her leaving this morning with Van Cleeve to see her father can't dampen the elation I feel.

Emma and I are getting married.

Shortly after Emma left I went to the jewelry store in downtown Romeo and chose a ring. The box is in my pocket. It wasn't the most expensive or the biggest stone. I tried to think about what she'd want, and when I saw the ring with rose and white gold entwined together with diamonds set like stars around it, I knew that it was meant for her. The jeweler was able to use their engraving machine to write in runes on the inside, *kiss me, I love you.*

Walking down the sidewalk of downtown Romeo I feel like

I'm grinning like a loon. I can't help it though, I feel so light and happy.

Two older women and a younger woman in a poodle skirt walk toward me down the sidewalk. They stare as they get close, and one of the old women elbows the younger one in the side.

"That's the pirate. I bet my liver, he's the pirate," she says excitedly.

"Shhh," says the young woman in the poodle skirt.

"Can you believe it, Petunia? I need a picture."

She pulls a phone out of her purse and tries to sneakily snap a photo of me. I stare in shocked surprise. The woman named Petunia smacks the other older woman with her purse and the young woman blushes furiously.

They're only a few feet up the sidewalk from me, a few doors down from the jewelry store.

I step aside for them to pass and nod my head in an awkward greeting.

"Good morning, ladies," I say.

"Morning," they chorus.

Then the photo-snatching one bares her teeth in a wide smile and says to the side, "Did you hear his accent? Panty-melting. Erma was spot on again."

"Shhh," says the young woman again.

Then they all beam at me as they scurry by. I watch them go, their heads together as they whisper furiously. The younger one looks back, sees I'm watching them, and turns away with an even brighter blush.

I shake my head.

What was that about?

Then I realize they mentioned that Erma character, the soul mate predictor. I smile, turn back toward the house and start to whistle. It looks like she was right. If I'd heard her prediction a few months ago I wouldn't have believed it. But now, I'm all in. I believe in fate and soul mates, one hundred percent.

Two hours later I'm in Sol's Cavern. As long as I'm here in Romeo, I may as well get to work. I've brought a digital camera, a tripod, a notebook, and my day pack with the usual gear. I place the camera in the center of the cavern and start taking photos. I'd like to take enough shots to have a vivid 3D recreation of the entire cavern. Then, I'd like high-res close-up photos for academic study. All told, I'll need to take hundreds of photos today.

When Emma gets back she and I can go to town hall together to register the find. I've been thinking about what she said last night. In the middle of the night, after a bought of lovemaking, she mentioned that she might like to stay in Romeo and create an educational archeology site from the cavern and the settlement. She described a museum, tours, an active dig site with opportunities for volunteers, educational programs for kids, ongoing research. She talked about finding funding from donors and working in conjunction with the town of Romeo. When she spoke, her cheeks grew pink and her eyes lit with excitement.

It was a beautiful sight.

I kneel down on the ground and look through the viewfinder at the runes on the cavern walls. My chest expands as I think about what a life in Romeo would look like. Not quite the same as Emma's original idea of us living in a tent at the edge of an archeology site in Central America. But...similar in many ways. There'd be me, her, and the joy of a new discovery every day.

I snap another picture of the runes and suddenly, I can

picture kids touring the site. And among them, my and Emma's children. They'll have my black hair, her smattering of freckles, and both of our adventurous spirits. We'll never have a moment of rest.

I grin at the thought.

Yes. I could definitely stay here.

In fact, maybe I'll buy the house I'm currently renting. There's no need for me to go back to New York.

Dom and I built our auction house so that within five years it would practically be able to run itself. I can step aside at any time and the business will still prosper. Yes, I think it's time to take a step back in pursuit of better things. Like a family.

I think of how Dom always laughed at me when I tried to save all the kids in every city we visited. Maybe if Emma and I start an educational site we can have a summer camp for disadvantaged youth. A summer in a beautiful place like Romeo, with people who believe in your future, could do a hell of a lot of good.

I like the idea so much that I decide to text Emma. I pull my phone from my pocket. No reception. I sigh. It's already after noon. I should grab lunch soon, I only have a granola bar, some trail mix and a water in my sack. I shrug and decide to crawl out of the cavern for a minute. I can send Emma a quick text and check in with her then come back in and finish up before heading into town.

I drop down to my stomach and start to army crawl through the tunnel. When I do, I see that there's someone standing at the entrance. I can see the thick legs of a man, clad in dark jeans and construction boots. I can see the bottom half of a flannel shirt. Then I notice something in his rough, meaty hand that's very familiar from the years I spent in the mine.

A detonator.

The hair on the back of my neck stands on end.

"Hey!" I shout. "Hey, I'm in here!"

I start to crawl quickly through the tunnel.

The man bends down and looks directly at me. "The Castletons send their regards," he says. Then he starts to sprint back toward the woods. My heart slams against my chest. I know what's coming. I'm not going to be able to crawl out in time. He's about to detonate some sort of explosive—likely a water-gel or an emulsion. Depending on how much he's used, the whole cavern may collapse around me. If I go forward I'll definitely be caught in the blast. I won't survive. If I go back, I may survive.

Decision made.

I scramble backward. When I make it back out of the tunnel, I sprint to the far side of the cavern. There's a boom, shaking, the rumble of falling rock, and a blast of dirt and debris flies out from the tunnel in a cloud that fills the cavern.

I drop to the ground and throw my arms over my head. Small rocks pelt me and cut into my skin. A large, jagged rock strikes my forearm and slices through my skin. I close my eyes against the sting of the dust in the air. I can't hear anything but a sharp ringing noise in my ears. I cough again, choke on the dust, then press my shirt over my nose and mouth. All the light has gone.

I stay down, crouched on the ground, and wait for any aftershocks. For another explosion. For the dust to settle.

Minutes pass. The ringing in my ears fades, although not completely. The dust settles and I can open my eyes and lower my shirt from my mouth. Slowly, I pull my cell phone from my back pocket and turn on the flashlight.

I choke back a curse when I see the tunnel. It's completely caved in.

I squat in front of it and stare at the pile of rocks blocking my only exit.

My stomach twists and I fight back the panic trying to rise. This isn't the same, I tell myself. This isn't the same. I'm not back in the mine. I'm not trapped. I can get out. I will.

In my mind I see the man looking at me, saying in a gravelly voice, "The Castletons send their regards."

The harsh sound of my breath is the only noise in the cavern.

I won't believe this of Emma. Not this time.

I know who did this. It wasn't her. I'll get out and I'll find her, tell her the whole truth, all of it. My revenge, my actions against her, what her father's done. I'll tell her everything and let her decide if she still wants me.

I just have to figure out how to get out.

But, having spent five years pulling stone out of tunnels, I have a better idea than most of how to succeed.

Two days.

It's been two days. I'm down to my last teaspoon of water. My throat burns. The granola bar and trail mix are long gone. My cell phone battery is dead. The bulb of my flashlight has been flickering the last hour and a half.

My hands are blistered, raw, and caked in blood from prying the rocks loose from the tunnel. I've used the camera tripod as a lever and my day pack as a sledge. But each time I pull a rock free, another falls from the wall into its place. The task is endless.

The pile of rocks in the cavern has grown and grown. I look up at the runes each time I pull a rock from the tunnel and place it in the pile. None of the poem was damaged in the explosion. Thank goodness. Emma would be devastated if it was.

Where is she?

She should've been back by now.

She should've wondered why I haven't called, where I am.

She should be here.

Where is she?

I won't doubt her again. I won't. But where is she?

I claw another stone free.

Three days.

I shove the final stone free from the mouth of the tunnel and fall forward onto the cool, mossy ground of the forest. I rest my cheek against the moss and breathe in the fresh scent. I lay on my stomach, with my arms spread out, my fingers grasping the ground. I take in the waning light of day. It's nearly dusk. I blink at the golden light on the bark of the trees.

I'm free.

My bag, my camera, they're all still in the cavern. But I don't want to crawl back in to retrieve them. I'll come later. With an excavation crew.

I push up onto my knees and take a deep breath. My head spins, so I shake it. I need water and food, then rest, in that order. But first, I need to find Emma. I climb to my feet and begin the mile hike out of the forest. When I arrive at the trail head, my Land Rover is still parked in the field at the edge of the dirt access road. It's covered in a fine layer of dirt and a few fallen leaves but isn't any worse for wear. I unlock it and plug in my phone.

I have a countless number of missed calls and texts.

I don't bother with them. Instead, I dial Emma.

I drum my fingers against the steering wheel. My head

swims, but the adrenalin rush of getting out of the cavern keeps my upright.

"Pick up, Emma," I say.

The phone continues to ring, until her voicemail picks up.

"This users mailbox is full…" a generic voicemail begins. I hang up and try calling again. The same message comes on. "This user's mailbox is full…"

I take a deep breath and try to think. My mind is fuzzy from lack of water, food and sleep. I decide to send her a quick text. I type in *call me.* It's the best I can come up with in my state. Then I drive back to the house.

I down water, slowly so as not to throw it back up. Eat food, even more slowly. Then I shower and change into clean clothes. Finally, I sit down in the kitchen with another glass of water and look at my phone. Nearly all the missed calls are from Dom.

I dial his number. He picks up on the first ring.

"Andrew. Thank goodness. Where have you been? Please tell me you haven't done anything rash. I cannot yank us out of this igniting minefield if you have."

I hold the phone to my ear, stunned, not sure how to respond.

"Andrew, are you there?"

I shake my head, try to clear it. "I'm here." I clear my throat. My voice is scratchy.

"Where have you been? It's been insane here. I swear, if you've gone off the deep end I will personally—"

I cut him off. "I've been trapped in a cave-in the last three days. Cut off without food or water. Left for dead. Courtesy of Edward Castleton. I need you to start from the beginning. I'm out of the loop."

Dom is silent for a moment, then he lets out a string of cuss words. I take a long sip of the water and wait for him to stop.

Finally, he's done. "I'm texting you a series of articles. You can read those. Long story short, you're all over the news as an unhinged stalker that spent years harassing and destroying Emma Castleton. The media's having a field day."

My blood runs cold.

"Where's Emma?" I say.

"Somehow they have a source giving all sorts of details. It's all circumstantial, but it doesn't look good. Our profits have tanked, customers are boycotting. Our lawyers are on it, we're preparing a libel suit, we're making a case to go after Castleton—"

"Where's Emma? Do you know where she is?" I demand. My throat is tight and the room is closing in around me. It's dark, the sun is down, and it's getting darker. I close my eyes and drag in a breath. "Dammit, Dom. If you know where she is, tell me."

He sighs, "I imagine she's with her fiancé."

I sit back down.

"Read the articles," says Dom. "Then call me and I'll review what the legal team has prepared so far."

He hangs up. I watch as the texts come through.

With a detached feeling, one of unreality, I click through them. It's all laid out. All my sins, and theories of sins I never committed, it's all laid out for the world to see. Neither Dom, nor Emma, nor Edward gave any comments to the press. There's speculation as to whether or not Suffolk Auction House can survive the scandal and speculation of criminal investigations into my past. Good luck. Everything I did, although morally questionable, was all completely legal. There is one last article. An engagement announcement for Justin Van Cleeve and Emma Castleton.

I drop my phone to the table. It clatters against the wood and then stills. I put my head in my hands.

So. That's it then.

A heavy weight settles on me and I don't know that I'll be able to shake it off.

It's funny. When I came to Romeo I had every intention of breaking Emma's heart. Instead, she broke mine. I was wrong. I was never her Visigoth, she's always been mine. My destruction. My ruin. My *more*.

My phone rings, it's Dom. I pick it up.

"What?" My voice sounds hollow.

He sighs. "Do we go after them? Libel. Defamation. The works. We can dig into Castleton's past. We all know the guy was not above board."

"No. Leave it." I say. There's a deep, aching weariness settling over me.

"I don't think we should let this stand—"

"Leave her alone," I say. I look down at the kitchen table and run my hand over its surface. Was it only a few nights ago that we were here together? I thought she was mine.

I close my eyes. I'm tired. So tired of it all.

"Leave her alone." I say again.

"Andrew. You alright? I can send up the plane. You can come back to NYC tonight."

"No. I'm fine. It's fine." I stand up from the table and walk up the stairs to the bedroom. "I need a night's sleep. Then I'll pull together a plan to deal with the fallout."

I stop at the door to the bedroom and look at the bed. The sheets are still rumpled from our last night together. I flinch as the moonlight catches the engagement ring box next to the bed.

"For what it's worth," says Dom, "I don't know what happened in your past, but I'm your friend and I'll stand by you. Alright?"

I tear my gaze away from the ring and walk back down the hall.

"I'll talk to you tomorrow," I say.

I hang up and wander into a guest room I've never been in before. I collapse onto the bed. Before I fall asleep I reach over to the nightstand and turn on the light.

The darkness is back.

17

———

I sit in a vinyl chair next to my dad's hospital bed. I've became intimately familiar with the hard cushion and creaky springs of this chair over the past four days. I've sat in it and slept in it for almost the entirety of my vigil. The only time I leave it are for quick trips to the bathroom or the cafeteria. My hand rests on the blanket next to my dad's arm, which is covered in bruises from needle pokes and IVs. He's asleep. It's nearly eight in the evening and out the small hospital window I can see the sky has faded to a dingy grayish blue. The beeping of the monitor and the smell of antibacterial solution have been ever-present, just like me in my chair.

This afternoon, the doctor came by and gave me hope that maybe tomorrow my dad will be able to move out of the ICU to a rehab facility. Then eventually back into his own home. This stroke was worse than any before. He said if there's another, my dad likely won't make it.

I've not left him. He hasn't regained much ability to communicate yet, and his physical mobility is even more limited than before. It's horrible. He did an awful, horrible, unforgivable thing. I want to rage at him, tell him I don't ever want to see him again. But I equally want to rage at him and tell him not to die. Not to leave me. I want the time to tell him how angry I am and how much he's hurt me, and the time for him to tell me why he did it. Or that he's sorry. I want the time to forgive him. But I know death doesn't work on a schedule.

"Em," my dad croaks out.

I look up from the bed at his face. He's awake and studying me. His eyes cloud, and I realize it's because I'm crying. I quickly swipe at the tears and give him a small smile.

"You're awake," I say.

He looks at my face, and I can feel where my skin is still wet. He lets out a shaky breath.

"Em," he says again. Then, so quiet and unsure I can barely hear it, "Sorry."

My face crumples and I turn away from him, keeping in my tears. I hold my breath and my throat tightens down. I won't cry. I won't.

Finally, I turn back to him. "You'll be fine," I say. "You'll be fine. You're going to be fine because you're horrible, and awful, and you've hurt me so much, and I need years to tell you that. Years to tell you how awful you are." I let out a shaky sob. "What were you thinking, Dad?"

He sighs and closes his eyes. Even speaking those two words drained him of energy.

"Anyway," I say, I reach over and lay my hand in his. "You have a lot to make up for. It's going to take years. I'll be married to Andrew."

At least I hope I'll be married to him. He hasn't returned my calls in days, and every time I phone his office they offer to transfer me to the legal department. I try not to think about what it means, because when I do all the logical conclusions scare me.

I continue talking to my dad. "I don't know if Andrew will be able to forgive you. Ever. If he can't, I'll stand by him. You understand?"

My dad doesn't open his eyes, and for a moment I think he's fallen back asleep, but then he slowly squeezes my hand.

"Good," I whisper. I gently pull my hand from his and lean back in my chair. I wrap my arms around myself and stare out the window as night falls.

JUSTIN SHAKES ME AWAKE. IT FEELS LIKE I WAS ONLY ASLEEP FOR A few minutes, but when I look at my watch it's been an hour. My heart leaps up into my throat and I quickly stand.

Justin volunteered to drive up to Romeo this morning. He's seen how worried the silence from Andrew has made me.

Justin told me this morning, point blank, that he believed Andrew had meant to seduce me then discard me and this was the discard moment. I disagreed. Then Justin claimed that the articles had perhaps put Andrew off, or the fake engagement announcement my dad had sent to the papers had put him into a sulk. I disagreed again.

I had to believe that something happened to him. Andrew was sick, or hurt. He wouldn't just not answer my calls or disappear on me.

Right?

"Did you find him?" I ask in a quiet voice, careful not to wake my dad.

Justin combs his fingers through his hair. He's rumpled and looks tired from taking his Saturday to drive nearly ten hours straight. He's gone into his office all week, but at night he's stopped by to check in on me and my dad. His mouth forms a hard line and I know his answer before he says it.

"No."

My stomach drops and I wrap my arms around myself.

"No, he wouldn't speak with you, or no you couldn't find him?"

Justin shakes his head. "The house he was renting is dark, and his car wasn't there. I asked around town. An old woman said she'd seen him a few days ago. But no one's seen him around in three or four days. Not since you left." He pauses. "Or since the article ran."

My shoulders slump. Is that what it comes down to? Is Justin right? Andrew left because he realized I'd found out what he'd done? Or that he still wanted revenge?

I shake my head. I know any logical person looking at outside facts would believe that, but I can't.

"I'm sorry," says Justin. "It's been a hard week."

I let out a half laugh, half sob. "You can say that again."

Justin looks over at my dad. "Any updates?"

My dad's cheeks are hollow and he looks frail.

"They said he should be out of here tomorrow. Then onto recovery."

Justin nods. "That's good." Then he clears his throat and puts his hands in his pockets. "I wanted to say something…" He trails off and I look at him closely, because I've never heard him sound so uncomfortable.

"What?" I tilt my head.

He takes his hands out of his pockets and then puts them back in again. What in the world?

"What is it?"

He shrugs. "I had a lot of time to think on the drive."

"Okay."

"You were right. We wouldn't make a good couple. I'm sorry if that put you in an awkward position."

I shake my head. "It didn't. It's okay."

He holds up his hand. "It did. I'm sorry. That was never my intent."

I smile, a little sadly. Then I reach out and squeeze Justin's arm.

"You can stay in the Romeo cabin as long as you need."

"Thank you." I squeeze his arm again then drop my hand.

After a few more minutes Justin heads out and I drop back into my chair. I lean my head back and the feeling I was holding back slowly creeps over me. Andrew's gone. He left Romeo. He's not answering my calls and he left the one place where I can find him.

I should've gone back earlier. Not that I could have. For the first three days I thought my dad wasn't going to make it. Today I sent Justin up. And now...I don't know.

I hear a vibrating noise in my overnight bag. It's my phone. Mostly I've been ignoring it because ever since the article and the engagement announcement came out, I've been bombarded with interview requests. Justin and I submitted a retraction to the announcement—it should run soon—but otherwise I've denied all media requests. That easiest way to do that is to ignore the calls and emails.

But since I haven't checked it in hours, I lean down and pull it out of my purse. I was right, the phone call was another interview request.

But my breath catches, because below that missed call are two missed calls from Andrew's cell and a text message.

Call me.

My heart skips a beat and then speeds up rapidly. I let out a sharp huff and hug my arms to myself. He's okay. He's okay. I didn't realize how worried I was for him until I saw that text. He's not sick or hurt. He's okay.

A smile breaks over my face.

Then it falters and a hint of nerves and doubt slips in. Where has he been and why hasn't he called? And the words *call me* are so terse and impersonal. What if he's calling to tell me to stop calling him, or his office, or…

I shake my head. There's no point in imagining things.

My finger shakes as I hit his number to redial, then I put the phone up to my ear. While it rings I walk across the room to the window, as far from my dad's bed as possible. I look out the window over the parking lot. The night is overcast and dark, and the parking lot lights barely penetrate the gloom. I shiver. Andrew still hasn't answered.

I'm about to give up, hang up, when the ringing stops.

"Hello?" he says, his voice is husky from sleep, I'm sure I woke him. At the sound of it I want to smile and cry at the same time.

"It's me…Emma," I say. Then I want to kick myself. Of course he'd know it was me.

I hear rustling then a bang and a sharp breath. Finally, "Emma?" He sounds more awake, but also more cautious.

"I got your text." Suddenly, I feel awkward. "To call you?"

"Oh. I…" He clears his throat and I hear more rustling.

"You saw the articles," I say. I feel as if my heart is in my throat. I wish I were there and I could see him and touch him. If I could only touch him then everything would be better.

"I did." He voice is curt and I flinch.

I stare at the darkness out the window. "My father gave the information to the newspapers. He…" I pause and lick my suddenly dry lips. "Andrew. I know what he did to you. I know everything."

"You do?" he sounds surprised.

"Yes. He told me. I'm sorry. You have no idea how sorry I am." I look at my blurry reflection and ache to reach out and touch him. Instead, I press my hand to the cold glass.

"If you knew why didn't you come?" he asks. His voice sounds distant, like it's breaking.

"My dad had a stroke. I couldn't leave him." But for some reason this answer makes me scared. Like it was the wrong thing to say. "Andrew?"

"Even after what he did?"

I look back at my dad, deathly still in the bed. "No. I mean, what he did was horrible. But I thought he was going to die. I didn't want him to be alone."

There's a noise on the other end, a harsh sound. I can't tell what it is, but it scares me. Then I realize that it's Andrew laughing. But it's a not a happy laugh, it's like his heart is breaking and he's laughing while it's happening.

"Andrew?" I whisper. Then, "I'm sorry."

"Right," he says. "Of course."

I continue on, ignoring the distance in his voice. "And I don't know if what the articles are saying is true or not. Or if my dad was right and you did purposefully destroy me. None of that matters to me. It doesn't matter. Do you understand?"

He quiets, and for a long moment there's silence. Then, "I understand. I hope you're happy, Emma."

A lump forms in my throat. Why did that sound like a goodbye?

"I am. I will be. If you just—"

"I wanted to let you know that I'll be registering the find tomorrow. But I won't be staying in Romeo. I doubt you'll see me again."

"What?" I cry. "Why?"

"You knew," he says. "You knew, Emma. And you didn't come."

My head spins and I press my forehead to the glass.

"Please."

"Goodnight, Emma."

He hangs up. I stay standing, the phone pressed to my ear, looking out at the dark.

~

I didn't sleep last night. I tossed and turned. Every few hours a nurse came in to take my dad's vitals. I watched, bleary-eyed and exhausted. Finally, morning light came, another gray, damp day. The sky is the color of unbleached soggy toilet paper.

I blink as the doctor strides in and informs me that my dad will be transferred this afternoon to the rehab facility we discussed. Everything is settled. I thank him and watch as my dad's breakfast tray is wheeled in. The smell of watery oatmeal and decaf coffee fills the room. I look over at my dad when he lets out a grunt.

"Morning," I say. I'm surprised that my voice comes out steady. It shouldn't. But oftentimes, as I know, the outside doesn't match what's happening within. I use the remote to help my dad raise his bed into a reclining position.

"I spoke to Andrew last night," I say.

My dad stills and I can tell that he's listening. I sniff and look away from his gaze. "He doesn't want to see me again." I turn back to my dad and give a small smile. "You may be happy to hear it."

My dad's bushy white eyebrows lower. He licks his lips and I can tell he wants to speak.

"Don't celebrate too much, Dad. I'm going to drive up to Romeo today. I'll convince him otherwise. I'm very convincing."

Over the last four days I've told my dad about Andrew, how

much good he's done, his charitable heart, his keen business mind. I think my dad understands that Andrew isn't the enemy. My dad has been his own enemy all along.

"I…" my dad begins, then stops. I lean forward and nod. "Hired…" He pauses and closes his eyes. There's a long pause and then he opens his eyes again. He looks frustrated.

"It's okay. I know."

He sighs. "Explo…bomb."

I stop. This is new. "You hired an explosion?"

"I…exploded…the…cavern."

"What? In Romeo?" My body floods with alarm. "My runic inscription in Romeo?"

I look down and see that my dad is clenching his right hand. He shakes with the effort of speaking.

"Why?" I ask.

"Car…Michael…inside."

Oh no.

Oh no, no, no.

I stare at my dad in horror. That's what he meant when he asked why I hadn't come if I knew what my dad had done. Was he trapped all those days he didn't answer my call?

I stand up. My dad looks at me with regret-filled eyes.

"I'm going, Dad."

He coughs. "Go," he says. He looks meaningfully at the door.

I grab my purse and rush out of the hospital.

I STARE AT THE DOCUMENT ON THE DESK AT TOWN HALL. IT'S THE official registration of the finding of the Lost Treasure. It was recorded this morning. I run my hand over the paper. The find is attributed to Emma Castleton. Me, and only me.

"Oh Andrew," I whisper.

He and the town hall secretary witnessed the document. It's all official. I found Romeo's Lost Treasure.

"It'll be all over town," says Ferran. "Everyone is going to go nuts." She leans against the desk and takes a sip of her coffee. I ran into her downtown, when I was frantically walking the sidewalks of Romeo trying to spot Andrew. I'd already checked the house—he wasn't there. I'd checked the woods—he wasn't there. The only thing I'd found was a rubble-strewn entrance to Sol's cavern.

I tried calling him on my train ride up, but his phone went straight to voicemail. So, I didn't know what to do except check all the restaurants and shops in Romeo in case he decided to stick around for a meal or something before leaving town for good. When I was in front of SweetStop, Ferran waved me down and told me all about my hunky soul mate and his registration this morning of our find.

What Ferran's saying finally breaks through my haze. "The police department will need to put up barricades and warnings. It's not safe to go in. There was an explosion."

"Wow," says Ferran. "Okay. I'll call them. I'm on it."

She gives me a happy grin and then heads back to her office. She's in a cozy glass-fronted room just down the hall.

I wave and head back outside. It's pretty clear that Andrew left this morning.

I stand on the sidewalk and look out over the brightly colored town. I'm at a loss. I don't know what to do or how to move forward.

I would never have guessed that Andrew would give up so easily. He spent five years fighting to get out of that mine, and then he spent another five years fighting to get me back. I smile and squint at the bright blue sky of Romeo. He might not see the last five years as him trying to get me back, but I do. He couldn't let me go. Just like I could never let him go.

I look around at the Official Town of Love, USA, and a plan begins to take shape.

I pull out my phone, scroll through my missed calls, find the reporter with the biggest network, and hit redial.

18

———

Andrew

I'm back in my office in NYC, towering over the city, with the glint of the Chrysler Building in the distance. It's been three days since I left Romeo. I'd thought I'd known pain and loss before. Unfortunately I didn't know what the hell I was talking about.

It's time to retire. Get out of business, buy a boat, and go live on a beach somewhere far, far away. No people, no newspapers, no internet, and no artifacts.

No reminders of Emma.

I look up as Dom strides in. He has on his favorite striped navy suit and he has a bounce in his step.

"Andrew," he says in greeting. He's entirely too chipper and jovial.

I sigh.

He walks to the bar and pulls out tonic from the fridge and grabs a glass. He looks around, like he's lost his keys, and scratches his head.

"Second shelf," I say. "When will you learn how to find things that are right in front of your nose?"

Dom gives me a sardonic look and pulls the gin from the second shelf. "Interesting question. I'd hoped the latest news would've improved your mood."

I look to the side. He must mean his communication with Van Cleeve. The Castletons have no lawsuit in the works and neither do we. There is a shaky, distrustful truce in effect.

"The Dutch masters collection went for twelve million," he says.

Ah. Of course, that's why he's here. I'd forgotten there was an auction today. I shake my head. There's no reason for me to stay a partner. I now realize that Emma was my only reason for pursuing this career.

What I actually want, what I needed, was her by my side, somewhere at a dig site, with a passel of kids. I hunch over to disguise the sharp pain in my chest.

"I want you to buy me out," I say. "There's no benefit to me remaining partner."

Dom casually walks over and leans against my desk. I expected a little more a reaction, but he just shrugs. "Your notoriety hasn't been all bad. This week we've been getting more attendance at our auctions. I think the press is increasing our company's name recognition."

Dom reaches over and flips through the papers on my desk. They're rough drawings of a plan for an educational dig site and museum. I put my hand over them and move them to the other side of the desk.

"To answer your question," he says, "maybe I'll start finding things right in front of my nose when you do." He lifts his glass to me in a sardonic toast and takes a sip.

I give him a flat stare. He shrugs and takes another sip.

There was no point in keeping my past from Dom any longer. He now knows everything that happened to me in the years before we met. He also knows what happened with the explosion and Emma's decision to choose her father over my safety.

A sharp pain hits me and I close the door on that thought.

"I heard from our contact in Mexico."

I perk up. We contacted a few security professionals we know and they set out a trace to find the man who detonated the cavern.

"And?"

The last I'd heard, they'd tracked his credit card purchases at gas stations and hotels.

He'd been driving south into Mexico.

Dom nods. "He wasn't the most savory character. He ran into some trouble at a border bar. Met the end of a knife. Apparently, he was flashing around wads of cash and the locals got greedy."

I glance at Dom and raise my eyebrows.

He holds up his hands. "Karma catches us all eventually."

Dom sets his glass down on my desk and stands. "I'll buy you out. I like money and refusing to buy you out is like refusing the lottery."

I swallow and then lean back in my chair. There's no satisfaction or relief, just a cold numbness. Almost the same feeling I had before leaving for Romeo. Then, Dom told me that Van Cleeve had proposed to Emma. I used that as an excuse to go after her.

Now, I don't have an excuse.

Yesterday, I read the retraction of Emma and Justin's engagement. Apparently, she's not marrying him after all. But there's still the fact that she knew that I was trapped in the cavern. She knew.

But does it matter? I want to say it does. But honestly, it scares me that it doesn't. Not really. I love her just as much. I want her just as much. I want to get down on my knees in front of her and beg her to have me. Maybe she didn't come because of the news articles, or because she was scared or confused. I don't know. I'm being torn apart inside from the desire to run to her and beg her to have me and the fear that she'll leave me again. In the dark.

Except I'm in the dark right now, aren't I?

I rub at my chest and try to ignore Dom pacing in front of my desk. Finally he stops and looks at me.

"I haven't seen you this bad since Cartagena. You look like hell," he says.

"Thanks. Appreciate the candor."

"You're welcome." He takes another swallow of his drink, then, "By the way, I have enough evidence on the Castletons to destroy them. The mine. The explosion. There's a paper trail a mile wide. Say the word. We can destroy them."

My jaw clenches as I think about what destroying Emma would look like.

"I never knew what drove you. Now I do. Let's finish this. You can finally get what you've worked so long for. What you've always wanted." Dom holds out a hand and waves it in the air as if a buffet of revenge is spread out before him. He smiles at me with a hard glint in his eyes, like he's looking forward to their destruction.

Inside, I rear back from the image, from the thought of hurting Emma, or yes...even her father.

"I told you to leave them alone," I growl. "Touch them and I will wring your neck. Are we clear?"

Dom steps back and smirks. His entire demeanor changes and his smirk transforms into a grin, as if he's just found a Van Gogh in an attic.

What the...?

"Perfectly clear." He looks down at his glass and stares at the ice cubes as if they hold the answers to the mysteries of universe. Then he looks up at me and pins me with a shrewd gaze, the one he uses when he's negotiating. I stiffen and narrow my eyes on him.

"What?"

"I'll buy you out of the partnership on one condition."

I sit up straight. He's shifted the conversation, but I like where it's gone. If he buys me out, I'll head south, find a beach and a boat. A deserted, lonely stretch of land.

"What's your condition?" I ask.

"You watch a news interview that aired last night from start to finish. I can pull it up right now. If you still want to sell after seeing it, then so be it."

I stare at him in consternation. This seems too easy. "What's the catch?"

"No catch. Just sit here and watch it."

I nod and open up my computer and the internet browser. "Fine. Deal."

He types in a big network interviewer and Emma's name. My skin prickles. "No." I don't want to sit here and watch a national interview with Emma. I don't know if I'll be able to handle seeing her face.

Dom looks at me and back at the link. "It's just an interview. I've never known you to be scared."

I stare at the screen.

"I'll leave you. Talk to you tomorrow," he says. He walks from the room with his glass.

I don't look up as he closes the door. Instead I stare at the interview title: *Emma Castleton Tells All.*

An icy dread spreads over me. I don't need to see this. Apparently, Dom thinks if I'm angry enough, I'll want to keep making money, keep building toward even more revenge. He really doesn't want me to leave. I sigh and pull my eyes from the screen.

I wonder exactly what Emma had to say. Does she talk about how betrayed she felt? Does she mention what we had? Or is it all business? Is she attempting to regain her standing in the field?

My eyes stray back to the link. I sit another five minutes, not thinking, just looking.

Finally, I swear and hit the link.

A video screen opens.

My first view of Emma feels like a fist to the gut. She's in a soft blue dress, her copper hair flows around her in waves, and her freckles stand out under the lights of the camera. She looks innocent and beautiful. Like the girl next door. There's no way that the whole nation won't fall under her spell and be howling for my blood. I clench my hands into fists and calm my breathing. I can't tear my eyes away from the screen.

The interview begins and Emma gives a shy smile. Her cheeks stain with a light blush. There are some initial light-volley questions to get the interview started. At first Emma stutters, and stumbles through her responses. But it's endearing and soon she's relaxed.

"I hear you recently made a new discovery? A Viking settlement in upstate New York." The interviewer, a reporter famous for his tête-à-têtes gives an overly toothy smile.

Emma's eyes brighten and a wide grin crosses her face. I lean forward and take in a sharp breath. She's so beautiful when she smiles.

"Not just me. Andrew Carmichael and I worked together on the find." She smiles shyly at the camera.

I stare, stunned, waiting for the inevitable interview-style evisceration. Why did she do that? I attributed one hundred percent of the find to her in the documentation. She didn't ever need mention me.

"Oh yes. Let's talk about Andrew Carmichael. There's been some interesting reports about him. What do they say? That he spent years maliciously sabotaging your career?" The interviewer leans forward, like he smells blood.

My stomach sinks. Here it comes. I turn my face away from the screen, back toward the window.

Emma gives a tinkling laugh. I jerk and look back at her. The male interviewer is enthralled and I have the urge to reach through the screen and punch him in the face.

"Would I be working with Andrew on a project if he did?" She gives the interviewer a condescending shake of her head, like he should know better than to ask silly questions.

I stare at her, enthralled. What is she doing?

"But surely there's some truth to the reports of his actions. He has a past."

Emma tilts her head, then slowly nods.

The reporter smiles in satisfaction. "So tell us, what did Andrew Carmichael do?"

I realize that my hands are starting to cramp, so I slowly release my clenched fists. The blood rushes back into my fingers.

"Well," says Emma, and she leans forward, as if she's about to share a secret. "This is hard to say."

"Go on."

My heart thunders in my chest.

"When I was twelve, I fell into a swollen river on one of my father's digs. I was drowning. Andrew dove in and pulled me out. He saved my life."

A sharp, painful exhale leaves my lungs. What is she doing?

"Then, when I was seventeen, our camp was attacked by a

violent militia. Andrew didn't think of his own safety, he saved my life, at great personal cost."

I stare at Emma, transfixed. She's looking straight at the screen. It feels like she's looking at me.

"You ask what Andrew did?" she says. "He saved me. Again and again. He's the best man I've ever known."

She's still looking at the camera, directly at me. I see the stars on her face and the sun in her eyes. I lift my hand and brush it over the screen.

I'll be. Dom didn't want to push me back to revenge, he's being his shrewd, conniving self and pushing me back to Emma.

The interviewer clears his throat and draws Emma's attention back to him. I curse him for distracting her.

"That's not how the news articles tell the story," he says.

She turns to him and lifts a delicately arched brow. "Hmm. Do you believe everything you read in the news?" She smiles conspiratorially at him.

The interviewer chuckles in surprise. "Touché, Miss Castleton. So, will you and Mr. Carmichael be working on more projects together? Can we expect more great finds?"

She smiles and her eyes crinkle, but I catch a hint of sadness in her expression. "There's nothing more in the world that I'd like better."

I sit, stunned, as the interview continues. The interviewer asks her about the bankruptcy, the fraudulent find, her dad's health—all the hot button topics, but Emma dances circles around him.

There's a warmth in my chest, and I realize that I was wrong, the darkness wasn't back, the light was just clouded over. I'm having a hard time pulling in a breath. She's incredible.

"Anything else you'd like to say?" asks the interviewer as he wraps up.

Emma nods and places her hands in her lap. "Yes. About our recent find."

"Go on."

"It's a beautiful Viking poem, from a husband to his wife."

"Romantic. Would you care to recite some of the lines?"

She nods, then twists her hands together. She stares into the camera again. And now I know, she is looking at me. She begins in a quiet voice that's barely audible in the microphone. "I love you so much that even fire seems cold. Kiss me, my love. Remember me. I remember you."

Suddenly, I stand and push back my chair. It skids across the floor.

"Wow. Those Vikings were romantic."

Emma nods and blushes. "If you want to learn more, you'll have to come to Romeo."

The interview begins to close, music cues in and the camera pans out. I don't wait to see the end. I sprint toward the door. I've got to go find my lost treasure.

19

Andrew

I take Suffolk Auction House's corporate jet to the private airport outside Romeo. The airport has a gray hangar, a runway, and a small office building. It's in the middle of a flat farm field, surrounded by a swath of trees. When we came in for landing, I could see the buildings of Romeo, the river, the mountain, and perhaps it was my imagination, but I also thought I could see the field where the settlement lies. The hour-long flight had me tapping my foot on the floor and drumming my fingers on the armrest nonstop.

I want to get to Emma.

Except, I know I can't just rush in there. I need to plan this. Do it right.

Once on the ground, I hire a car service, a black Cadillac with an older gentleman driver, and head into town. It's a short fifteen-minute drive, but I'm impatient. On the way, my phone rings. It's Van Cleeve. I grip the phone in my hand a lot tighter than necessary. I haven't spoken to him since he drove Emma away.

In fact, I can't think of any good reason for him to be calling. Unless, something's happened to Emma?

I answer quickly. "What is it?" I snap.

Van Cleeve lets out a surprised chuckle. "I've always admired your brass, Carmichael. You really don't care what people think of you, do you?"

Not true. I care a whole helluva lot what Emma thinks of me.

"What is it?" I grate out again. I want to ask if Emma is alright, but I don't.

He sighs and mumbles something to himself. "I was calling as a favor," he says, and I'm surprised to find that I believe him.

"Go ahead."

"I'm sorry to hear about the explosion," he begins.

"Accidents happen," I say warily.

He lets out a poorly concealed scoff that makes me wonder how much he knows.

"Be that as it may, for the four days you were MIA, Emma was frantic. I drove all the way up to Romeo looking for you, just to reassure her. She couldn't believe that you'd just disappear. She couldn't fathom that you wouldn't contact her. She didn't know where you were. Do you understand what I'm saying?"

I sink back into the leather seat of the Cadillac. "I hear you," I say. It's nothing short of what I concluded flying into Romeo. Emma didn't know about the explosion. On the phone, when she said she knew, she must've been talking about her dad's part in the attack ten years ago.

"You hear me?" He sounds as close to exasperated as Van Cleeve can come to the emotion.

"Thanks for the call," I say.

He swears. "If you don't get your ass to Romeo and do right by Emma, so help me—"

"Appreciate the call," I say. I give a half-smile. Van Cleeve is still cussing me out. Maybe someday, when he gets over his inappropriate crush on my soon-to-be wife, Van Cleeve and I will be friends. He lets out another string of cusses. I smile. Or not...probably, we won't be friends.

I chuckle.

"Will you stop laughing and get on your private jet and... you're already there, aren't you?" he asks.

"Talk to you later," I say.

I hang up on him mid-sentence. I grin as the driver pulls into downtown.

"Here's fine," I say.

We slow in front of town hall. I have a lot to do in the next few hours.

It took more than a few hours.

Even with unlimited funds, a work crew of a dozen men, construction machinery, and half the town working to help my goal, it still took six hours to get everything ready.

The gravel crunches under the rental car's tires as I pull into the drive in front of Emma's cabin. Apparently, it belongs to Van Cleeve, but I choose to ignore that fact. I step out of the car and breathe in the pine-scented air. Sunset is in forty-five minutes.

I didn't check to see if Emma was here before coming. Jessie, the town librarian, assured me she was. I ran into Jessie and one of the older ladies she was with the other day, outside of town hall. When I mentioned that I could use some help, the old lady started cackling and rubbing her hands.

"We get to meddle," she crowed happily.

Within thirty minutes, she had half of Romeo gathered and working together to help me win Emma. I was awed and thunderstruck at the generosity of this town for a near stranger.

I clear my throat and loosen the collar of my shirt, suddenly nervous. There's a lamp on inside the cabin and I can hear classical music coming from the radio. It's so Emma. She loves everything historic. I rub a hand over the back of my neck and pause at the door.

I realize I'm afraid to knock. In the whirlwind of preparations today, I never once paused to think about what I'd do if Emma said no.

What if I misunderstood the message in her interview and she didn't actually want me to come? What if instead of saying come back to me, she was saying goodbye?

I stare at the faded and scratched blue paint of the wood door. I shift uncomfortably and the edge of the engagement ring box in my pocket digs into my thigh.

What if she turns me away? If she says we've hurt each other enough?

What if I'm wrong?

The sun falls closer to the horizon. It's nearing dusk. A ray of the sun shines through the leaves and lights across my face. The beam is a brilliant golden white.

I let out all the fear and tension.

It's going to be okay.

I hold up my hand and knock on the door.

20

I HAVE TO ACCEPT THE FACT THAT THE INTERVIEW DIDN'T WORK. Andrew hasn't come, hasn't called…hasn't anything.

I sit in the old recliner chair in the cabin, my arms wrapped around my legs and my chin resting on my knees. Everything's quiet except for the radio playing Vivaldi. On the TV tray next to me is a grant proposal I'm working on. Even if Andrew doesn't come, I want to move forward with my project. I'm going to create a living history museum and active dig site for people to explore for generations. I want others to feel the love and the awe that I felt when I first saw Sol's Cavern with Andrew.

That's a gift I can give.

I sigh and lean back in the recliner. It creaks and groans in protest.

I wonder where he's at right now. I wonder what he's doing, what he's thinking and feeling. I wonder if he misses me.

I sigh.

I wish I could go back in time and change the past. I'd start with the night we found *The Heart*. I wouldn't stay hidden in the bushes. I would've fought. Then, for the next five years, I would've torn apart heaven and earth to find him. If I didn't find him, then when he finally returned I would've married him that day. Demanded it. I wouldn't have left him and I wouldn't have let him go.

I stare at the wall of travel knickknacks and the old TV. Then I realize that's my answer. The interview wasn't my last hurrah. It was just the beginning. Just because I can't change the past doesn't mean I can't change my future.

I'm going after him.

I'll find him. Wherever he is.

I jump up from the couch and run to my suitcase. I throw on the cleanest, least scruffy pair of shorts I have and a billowy top. I finger comb my hair then grab my phone, purse and suitcase. I can call a cab and head to the bus stop. The first place to look is NYC, at Suffolk Auction House headquarters.

Determination fills me. I won't give up.

I rush to the door. Just as I'm about to throw it open, someone knocks.

It's Andrew.

I'm stunned. No words come out. I was prepared to chase him around the world, and here he is at my door.

"You're leaving?" he asks. His mouth compresses and he looks...concerned. He eyes the suitcase in my hand.

I give him a wobbly smile. He's here. *He's here.*

My eyes rove over his features, taking him in like a drink of water in the scorching desert. The sun bathes him in gold, painting his skin a luminescent hue. He's in jeans, boots and a t-shirt—his explorer look. The scars on his arms are visible and my heart gives a sharp pang. He's not hiding anymore. His dark eyes are wary, I'd say almost fearful, but I've never known Andrew to be fearful a day in his life. Except...when he thought he was going to lose me. I let out a sharp breath and blink up at him. Does he think he's lost me?

He clears his throat and runs his hand over his mouth and down his jaw. "Are you going?"

His eyes shift to my suitcase and purse. I shake my head. My heart thunders in my ears. "No." I drop the suitcase and my purse and step back into the cabin. "Do you want to come in?"

His eyes shift to a darker shade and I can't read whether it's relief I see or fear. He closes his eyes for a second and I take the time to study his face. He looks tired. Like he hasn't slept in days. There are dark circles under his eyes and the scar over his eyebrow seems more pronounced. Then I notice that he has fresh cuts on his face, his hands, and his arms. It's from the explosion—my dad. I flinch, and when I do, he opens his eyes and sees my reaction to him.

When he does his expression shutters and he turns his face away. He thinks that I'm flinching away from him.

Never.

Well, now's the time to start living my future—the one where I run to what I want.

"Andrew?"

He looks back at me and gives a small smile. "I saw your interview."

My mouth goes dry. "What did you think?"

His gaze heats, and he can't hide the yearning in his expression. Not from me. The warmth that started when I found him at the door grows and grows.

He looks to my mouth, the freckle above my lip, then into

my eyes. "I thought you were radiant. More radiant than the sun."

Joy bursts inside me. I fling myself into his arms. He lets out a surprised huff and catches me.

Then he's kissing me, and I'm kissing him back. I jump up and wrap my legs around his waist and my arms around his neck. He holds me up and crushes me to him.

"Emma," he whispers against my mouth. "My Emma."

I clutch him and nod. "Yours."

Then, instead of continuing the kiss he pulls away and looks into my eyes. I give a dissatisfied squeak. But he slowly pulls me away from him and gently sets me on my feet.

"I was hoping you'd come with me," he says. He nods his head back toward the door. There's an eager, hopeful expression on his face.

"Where?"

He smiles. "It's a surprise."

I can't help but give an answering smile. "Will we be gone long?"

He shakes his head no.

"Is it far?"

Again he shakes his head no, but his smile grows.

"Alright."

He takes my hand and leads me out the door. There's a rental car in the drive. He holds the passenger door for me and then we're off.

He pulls onto the country road and heads away from town, toward the forest. Honestly, it doesn't matter where he takes me, as long as I'm with him.

I reach over and rest my hand on his. He looks at me in surprise and then gives me a warm, satisfied look. One I want to see on his face every day for the rest of his life. Less than a minute into the drive he pulls into the fire access road and heads toward the meadow.

I swallow down a nervous lump in my throat. He's taking me to the cavern. I've only been back once, days ago, when I was frantically looking for him. It was rubble-strewn and I haven't had the heart to go back since. I don't know why he wants to show it to me.

Maybe to help me understand what my dad's done?

Andrew parks at the tree-line and gets out of the car. The sun has nearly set and the sky is tinged purple and denim blue. We have maybe fifteen minutes of light left. There are swallows flying over the field in swooping formations, catching their insect dinner.

Andrew comes around and opens my door then helps me out. Even when I'm standing he doesn't let go of my hand. He starts to walk toward the trail head. We're not far from the cavern, but...

I pull to a stop. Andrew looks back at me.

"I've seen the explosion. You don't have to take me. It's awful. I'm sorry. I didn't know he did it. I never imagined he'd do the things he did. I didn't know you were trapped. I didn't—" Once I start, I can't stop. All my fear for him, the fear that I felt after I found out about the explosion, even though he was already free, comes pouring out.

Andrew wrinkles his brow and shakes his head. "No. Emma. That's not why we're here."

"What?" I stop and stare at him.

"I'm not here to show you a ruin."

"You're not?"

He gives a small, secret-filled smile. "Definitely not."

After that I'm quiet as he tugs me quickly through the darkening forest. We make it to the mouth of the cavern minutes before sunset. I stop, completely shocked by what I see.

"What? How?"

All of the rubble is cleared and piled into a large stone stack ten yards from the entrance. There's a construction vehicle parked next to the rock pile.

Andrew gives a sly smile and shrugs. "When you offer a hundred times the going rate, people are motivated to work fast."

I let out a surprised laugh.

"You're happy?" he asks. Suddenly, he looks nervous.

I press my hand to his cheek. "Happier than you can know."

He turns his mouth to my hand and presses his lips to my palm. Then he pulls away and his eyes are heated. "Then in you go," he says.

I look at him in surprise. "Are you sure?"

I know how he feels about the dark, and he just spent four days trapped in that cavern.

"More sure than you can know." He gives me a look full of meaning and unspoken words. Then, "Go on." He nods at the cavern.

I will, but before I do, I stand on my tiptoes and place a quick kiss on his lips. Then I drop to my knees and crawl into the cavern. The entrance is taller by a good two feet. It's no longer smooth, but jagged. The explosion did quite a bit of damage. I hear Andrew coming in behind me, then feel his hands brushing against my heels. The cavern smells different than before, sweet and floral rather than earthy. I don't know what to think about that.

Ahead, the room is dark. I imagine we're about a minute until the sunset will bathe the room in golden light. I reach the opening and stand up. Andrew's right behind me.

He comes and stands next to me.

When he does, the sun hits the tunnel and light floods in.

I gasp.

The room lights up and I see what Andrew wanted me to see, and exactly how much he loves me. The cavern is full of white roses. There are hundreds of them in crystal vases, and thousands of white rose petals covering the ground in a fragrant, soft, carpet. The sunlight hits the crystal vases and prism rainbows dance along the cavern walls. I spin in a circle and take it all in. I've never seen anything so beautiful in my life. I feel like I'm in a fairytale.

"Andrew, it's..." I trail off. I've spun back around, and instead of standing next to me, Andrew's kneeling on the ground.

I stop and my heart kicks against my chest. He smiles up at me, but his mouth shakes and his eyes are filled with questioning hope. I want to drop to my knees next to him and wrap him in my arms, but instead I hold still as he takes both my hands in his.

He swallows, and I gently squeeze his hands and hold back my tears.

"I had what I was going to say memorized." His voice is rough from emotion and unshed tears. "But I've forgotten it all." He shrugs and gives me the rueful smile that I love. "I wanted to give you the roses that you love. And the gold of the sun. And rainbows as beautiful as all the gems buried in the earth. But most of all, I wanted to give you me." His mouth trembles again and he gives me a look, like perhaps giving me himself was the smallest gift of all. He still doesn't realize how much he means to me.

I drop down to my knees in front of him. The rose petals cushion the ground so it feels like I'm kneeling on a plush carpet.

"I've never, not ever, in all my life, wanted anything else," I say.

He closes his eyes, and his shoulders relax. "Thank you, God," he breathes.

When he opens them again, I'm smiling at him.

The sunlight is still flowing into the cavern, the roses and petals sparkle like snow on a sunny day, and little rainbows flicker on the walls.

He peers at me, like he's reassuring himself that I'm really here. Then, "I did a lot of what the newspaper article said. I did try to ruin you."

I nod, once, in acknowledgement. "I know."

He swallows nervously. "I'm the reason you lost your family business, your home, your reputation. I wanted you to lose everything. I wanted you to feel as much pain as I did."

A single tear falls from the corner of his eye and tracks down his face.

I reach up and catch the tear, wipe it away. "I know," I say again.

His shoulders shake and he drops his head. I kneel forward, wrap my arms around him. I never cared about any of it, I only cared about him. I press my lips to his face, his neck, his brow.

"Forgive me," he weeps, and my heart breaks.

"You came home. That's all that matters to me. You came home." I wrap him in my arms and keep repeating that phrase. He came back to me. Finally, he hears me. He leans into me and presses me into the rose petal-strewn floor. The light is almost gone, but there's still enough for me to see the love in his eyes. He covers my body and presses into me.

"Will you love me?" he whispers. He presses his mouth against mine and I taste his tears, but also his hope. "Will you?"

I lean up into him, rock my hips against him. "I never stopped."

He lets out a defeated groan as I pull his clothing off and strip him naked. I pull my own clothing off and settle back into the rose petals. They're silky and cool on my skin. Andrew rises above me, props his arms around my shoulders and looks down at me as if I've given him the best gift in the whole world. He spreads my knees with his legs, opens me to him, then settles himself at my entrance. He rests his forehead to mine and grasps my hands.

"I love you," he says.

"I love you," I cry out. He thrusts into me, pushes me into the bed of rose petals. He cries out into my mouth and I cling to him. He buries himself in me, deeper and deeper as I am swept up in a sensation so amazing, so earth-shattering, that I don't have any word for it—expect *love*.

Andrew drops down next to me and pulls me into his arms. He's breathing hard and I rest my head on his chest and listen to his heart race. He runs his fingers through my unruly hair and I run my hands along his shoulders.

Then, he stiffens and shifts me down to the floor.

"Stay there," he says. He kisses my forehead and goes back to his clothes. When he returns, he kneels next to me.

The light is nearly gone and I can only see his outline. But in his hand I can make out the shape of a jewelry box. I sit up and lean into him. When I do, the rose petals send up a floral scent.

"Come here," he says.

I smile as he pulls me into his lap and wraps his arms around me. "I'm not letting you get away," he growls into my hair.

I turn and kiss his mouth.

"Do you have something to ask me?" I settle back into his chest.

"No," he says.

I turn to look at him, taken completely by surprise.

He rubs his nose against mine. "I'm not going to ask. I'm going to tell you. Emma Castleton, you are my soul mate, my one true love, I've known it for nearly twenty years and so have you. You're mine and I'm yours. Nothing can keep us apart. You're going to marry me. You're going to be my wife."

"Yes," I say. "And I'm not asking either. You're mine. Only mine."

I wrap my arms around his chest and hold him tight. He opens the box and pulls out a gold ring that barely glints in the fading light.

"With this ring, I thee wed," he whispers. He takes my left hand and slips it on my finger. As he does, the world shifts, and I feel as if everything has come into alignment.

"Now you're my wife," he says.

"And you're my husband," I agree. Because this is exactly how they wed in many ancient cultures, with bodies and hearts joined in love, and with a promise of forever. That's all I've ever wanted. And forever starts right now.

EPILOGUE

I CURL INTO ANDREW'S SIDE. AN INVOLUNTARY BUBBLE OF laughter comes up. He yawns and looks over at me wryly. It's not quite six in the morning, and neither of us got much sleep last night.

"What are you laughing at?" he asks. He tugs on a lock of my hair and there's a new lightness and happiness to him. He's completely free of the past. So am I.

Except the good parts we wanted to keep—our love for each other.

I snuggle closer to him under the covers of the bed at our new home. Andrew bought the beautiful old house he was renting in downtown Romeo as a wedding gift. I love it. We were married yesterday, and this afternoon we're flying to Andrew's private island for our honeymoon.

"Well?" he asks.

I drop a kiss on his lips. "I was only thinking of how unhappy Mrs. Charles, the bookstore owner, was that we didn't have our wedding on your island."

He grins at me. "She didn't like the meadow wedding with the cavern tour?"

I snort.

"That shows a sad lack of an adventurous spirit," he says.

I nod in agreement. "Absolutely. And you know how I love adventure. In fact, I can count at least a dozen new positions... er, places you took me last night."

Andrew lets out a deep, rumbly laugh that hits me down low and causes a responsive clenching. "There are plenty more places to travel," he promises.

He rolls on top of me and brings the blankets with him. We're in a cocoon, wrapped up together. He leans down and kisses me.

"You're happy?"

"Ecstatic," I say.

We're breaking ground on the settlement dig next month, and plans for the museum are underway. Andrew has pulled back from his role in Suffolk Auction House, instead concentrating on our joint project—Romeo's first historical living museum and dig site.

We had the wedding in the grassy meadow, right on top of the buried Viking settlement. We invited all our new friends in Romeo, and all our old friends, Justin, Dominic, and my dad and Linda. My dad has recovered more of his speech and mobility, and after the wedding he asked to speak with Andrew alone. After they came back, they both seemed more at ease with each other.

"By the way, what did my dad say yesterday?" I ask.

Andrew rolls to his side and pulls me into him. He presses a kiss into my hair. "Not much. That he accepted any censure, recompense, or reparation I required. He acknowledged everything he'd done and told me I was welcome to do whatever I wanted to him."

I pull in a breath. "What did you say?"

He rubs a strand of my hair between his fingers. "Did you know, sometimes your hair shines just like a copper coin from Rome circa 68 BC?"

I smile at him. I'll never get tired of him. But, "Don't distract me. What did you say?"

The edges of his eyes crinkle with mischief, and he drops my hair. "I said that the only thing I wanted as recompense was your happiness. And if he admitted that I was integral to your happiness, then we wouldn't have a problem."

I hug him close to me and smile into his shoulder. "You are the best man I know."

He puts his hand under my chin and lifts my eyes to his. "Does that mean I get a present?"

I laugh. "Yes. A thousand presents. But maybe one special present today..."

I drift off mysteriously and Andrew looks at me with interest. "Yes?"

I lean in and whisper in his ear. "You know how you dreamed of a dig site, and tours, and kids programs, and maybe a passel of our own kids running around too?"

He grows still and then slowly nods.

"You get your wish," I whisper. I reach out and take his hand and place it on my abdomen.

He turns his face to mine and his eyes are wide. "You mean...?"

I nod.

He doesn't move, and for a moment I'm worried that he's not happy. Then I realize that there are tears in his eyes.

"Happy?" I ask.

"How could I not be? All my wishes just came true."

Then he leans in and kisses me, and the rest of the world disappears as the sun rises and bathes the room in light.

208

THE END

KISS ME
LOVE ME

GET A BONUS EPILOGUE

Want more Andrew and Emma? Get an exclusive bonus epilogue for newsletter subscribers only.

When you join the Sarah Ready Newsletter you get access to sneak peaks, insider updates, exclusive bonus scenes and more.

Join Today!

www.sarahready.com/newsletter

A NOTE FROM THE AUTHOR

Dear Reader,

In years past I dug up fossils, traveled to out of the way archeological sites, crawled into barrows, descended into a jungle-hidden watery cave that in centuries past was known as the mouth of the underworld, and explored ancient ruins. My love of digging up the past landed me a laboratory job and lots of adventures.

Both the cenote and the Heart of the Empress are fictional, but they are based on my experience traveling on horseback deep into the jungle, far beyond roads and civilization. Likewise, the Viking Settlement in Romeo is fictional (as Romeo is a fictional town), but based on modern findings of Viking settlements in Canada.

The poem in Sol's Cavern is based on a compilation of actual Runic Inscriptions from Bergen, Norway circa AD 1150-1350. You can find a translation of the runic inscriptions online. It's also true that graffiti was a favorite pastime of bored Vikings, as well as other people groups of the past. The sampling of historical graffiti shows that humans have always been funny, proud, lovesick, or crude. Take your pick!

I hope you enjoyed Emma and Andrew's adventure. I'm so glad I could bring them to Romeo. And thanks for sticking with me while I fudged archeology/history a bit for some fictional fun.

Thank you for reading!

All the best,
Sarah Ready

ABOUT THE AUTHOR

Author Sarah Ready writes contemporary romance and romantic comedy. Her books have been described as "euphoric", "heartwarming" and "laugh out loud". Her debut novel *The Fall in Love Checklist* was hailed as "the unicorn read of 2020".

Before writing romance full-time Sarah had lots of fun teaching at an Ivy League. Then she realized she could have even more fun writing romance. Her favorite things after writing are adventuring and travel. You'll frequently find her using her degree at a dino dig site, crawling into a cave, snorkeling, or on horseback riding through the jungle – all fodder for her next book. She's lived in Scotland, Norway, Portugal, Switzerland and NYC. She currently lives in the Caribbean with her water-obsessed pup and her awesome family. You can visit her online at www.sarahready.com

Stay up to date, get exclusive epilogues and bonus content. Join Sarah's newsletter at www.sarahready.com/newsletter.

ALSO BY SARAH READY

Stand Alone Romances:

The Fall in Love Checklist

Hero Ever After

Josh and Gemma Make a Baby

Soul Mates in Romeo Romance Series:

Chasing Romeo

Love Not at First Sight

Romance by the Book

Love, Artifacts, and You

Find these books and more by Sarah Ready at:

www.sarahready.com/romance-books

Sign up to receive bonus content, exclusive epilogues and more at:
www.sarahready.com/newsletter